Clint heard a hammer cock, and as Adrian Webster came out the door, one shot. Then the sound of a bullet striking flesh. Clint stepped to the side, went down to one knee, and reached behind him, beneath his jacket, for the New Line. When Frank Ellington came out the door, he stopped as Webster fell in front of him. Confused, Ellington looked at Clint just as the New Line came out and lined up on him. Eyes wide, Ellington went for the gun in his belt . . .

WITHDRAWN

THE GUNSMITH

336
BAD BUSINESS

J. R. ROBERTS

JOVE BOOKS, NEW YORK

THE BERKLEY PUBLISHING GROUP
Published by the Penguin Group
Penguin Group (USA) Inc.
375 Hudson Street, New York, New York 10014, USA
Penguin Group (Canada), 90 Eglinton Avenue East, Suite 700, Toronto, Ontario M4P 2Y3, Canada
(a division of Pearson Penguin Canada Inc.)
Penguin Books Ltd., 80 Strand, London WC2R 0RL, England
Penguin Group Ireland, 25 St. Stephen's Green, Dublin 2, Ireland (a division of Penguin Books Ltd.)
Penguin Group (Australia), 250 Camberwell Road, Camberwell, Victoria 3124, Australia
(a division of Pearson Australia Group Pty. Ltd.)
Penguin Books India Pvt. Ltd., 11 Community Centre, Panchsheel Park, New Delhi—110 017, India
Penguin Group (NZ), 67 Apollo Drive, Rosedale, North Shore 0632, New Zealand
(a division of Pearson New Zealand Ltd.)
Penguin Books (South Africa) (Pty.) Ltd., 24 Sturdee Avenue, Rosebank, Johannesburg 2196,
South Africa

Penguin Books Ltd., Registered Offices: 80 Strand, London WC2R 0RL, England

This is a work of fiction. Names, characters, places, and incidents either are the product of the author's imagination or are used fictitiously, and any resemblance to actual persons, living or dead, business establishments, events, or locales is entirely coincidental.

BAD BUSINESS

A Jove Book / published by arrangement with the author

PRINTING HISTORY
Jove edition / December 2009

Copyright © 2009 by Robert J. Randisi.
Cover illustration by Sergio Giovine.

ISBN: 978-0-515-14724-7

JOVE®
Jove Books are published by The Berkley Publishing Group,
a division of Penguin Group (USA) Inc.,
375 Hudson Street, New York, New York 10014.
JOVE® is a registered trademark of Penguin Group (USA) Inc.
The "J" design is a trademark of Penguin Group (USA) Inc.

PRINTED IN THE UNITED STATES OF AMERICA

10 9 8 7 6 5 4 3 2 1

ONE

When Clint Adams stepped off the train onto the platform in San Francisco, he missed having Eclipse underneath him. He still preferred horseback to trains. When he stepped out onto Market Street and climbed aboard the cable car, he missed his horse even more. How much longer, he wondered, until horses were totally obsolete? That wasn't something he wanted to think about.

In San Francisco Clint's location of choice was usually Portsmouth Square—or just off it. He had several friends who ran hotels and gambling halls in and about the square, but that wasn't what he was in town for this time. He got off the cable car and walked to a hotel on Powell Street, checked in, and went to his room. It wasn't a flophouse, but it certainly wasn't on a par with the hotels around Portsmouth Square.

It wasn't even as comfortable as the hotel in Chicago had been . . .

When he got the telegram summoning him to a meeting in Chicago, he was in his hotel room in Labyrinth with a saloon girl named Maisie Wilson. Maisie was a busty blonde in her early thirties who was just passing through Labyrinth. She'd taken a job at Rick Hartman's saloon for a few weeks, and she and Clint also decided to spend some of that time together in his room, in his bed.

On this morning he had her on her hands and knees, lovely big, pale butt hiked in the air so he could slide his cock into her from behind. He had just pierced her to the hilt when there was a knock on the door.

"Oh, Jesus," she said, "don't answer it, Clint." She actually tightened herself around him, forbidding him to withdraw. That wonderful control of her muscles convinced him.

From the bed he shouted, "Who is it?"

"Uh, telegram came for you, Mr. Adams," the desk clerk said.

"Slide it under the door!" he yelled.

"Uh, yes, sir."

He took firm hold of Maisie's hips and went back to what they were doing . . .

"What is it?" she asked, breathlessly.

After they were finished, he had walked to the door and picked up the telegram from the floor. He opened it, read it, then folded it again and put it in one of the chest drawers for later.

"Nothing important," he said, getting back in bed with her. She cuddled up next to him, reached for his cock, and began to stroke it. Before long he was long and hard again, and she was ready.

"You sure it wasn't important?" she asked, as he positioned himself between her chunky thighs. In his old age Clint was finding himself more and more preferring women with meat on their bones.

He pressed the head of his penis to her moist pussy and said, "Not as important as this," just as he glided into her.

"Who's the telegram from?" Rick Hartman asked him, later.

"Jim West."

"The mystery man."

"Mystery man?"

"I've never met him," Hartman said. "Have you?"

"Of course I've met him," Clint said. "He's my friend."

"Yeah, okay," Hartman said. "What's he want?"

"He wants me to come to Chicago," Clint explained, "check into a hotel, and meet with someone in Washington Square Park."

"Meet with who? Him?"

"I don't know."

"And you're gonna go?"

"I am," Clint said.

"Why?"

"Well . . . the telegram is from Jim West, right?" Clint said.

"And when he calls you run?"

"Rick, there are four men who could send me a telegram like that . . . no, sorry, five men who could send me a telegram like that and I would respond to it, no questions asked. Or come running, as you said."

"Lemme guess," Rick Hartman said. "Jim West, Bat Masterson, Wyatt Earp, um, oh, yeah, Talbot Roper, and . . . who?"

Clint smiled at his friend and said, "That would be you, Rick. You."

When Clint arrived in Chicago, he'd checked into a hotel on East Chicago Street near Washington Square Park. Even then he'd found himself missing the time he spent on horseback. But the request for him to come to Chicago was urgent and did not allow for him to ride there from Texas.

He was on the second floor, and as he looked out the window he marveled at how Chicago was growing. It was too big—too many high buildings, too many people, too many things like elevators and telephones.

He had a meeting set for later that day, and after the meeting he hoped to leave Chicago and get back to the West. He had no idea the meeting would take him directly to San Francisco for another meeting.

But first, the Chicago meet . . .

He freshened up, left his hotel, and walked down the street to Washington Square Park. He didn't know who he was going to be talking to, so his instructions were to simply walk until he was contacted. If he wasn't contacted, he was to come back the next day, at the same time, and walk some more. He was guaranteed the meet would take place either the first day or the second.

He was hoping for the first.

TWO

Clint only had to walk about a mile before a man approached him. He recognized the man immediately. It was not James West, of the Secret Service.

It was William Pinkerton.

Since the death of Allan Pinkerton in 1884, William and his younger brother, Robert, had been running the Pinkerton Detective Agency.

Pinkerton extended his hand.

"Hello, Mr. Adams."

"William." The two men shook hands.

"Can we walk?" Pinkerton asked.

"Sure," Clint said. "I'm enjoying the exercise."

"I'm sorry for all the secrecy," Pinkerton said, as he fell into step with Clint. "We really didn't want anyone to see you coming into the office."

"We?"

"My brother, Robert, and myself," William said.

"So Robert knows about this meeting?"

"Robert, me, Jim West . . . and now you."

"And how many know what this meeting is actually about?"

"Robert, Jim, myself . . . and soon, you."

"As soon as you tell me, right?"

"That's correct."

William was tall, dark-haired, in his forties, and easily matched strides with Clint as they walked through the park. It was spring, and mild, but he was wearing a long coat. Clint wondered if he was armed beneath it. Because he was walking the streets of Chicago, and not Dodge City, Clint had left his holstered Colt back in the room. Instead, he had his little Colt New Line tucked into his belt at the small of his back.

"Well," Clint said, "I'm all ears."

"What?"

"It's just something I heard once," Clint said. "It means I'm listening."

"Adams, I know you weren't fond of my father."

"I didn't like him," Clint said, "but I respected old Allan."

"When he died," William said, "my brother and I suspected foul play."

"That makes sense," Clint said, "what with everything he did in the war and all the criminals he'd put away since. But . . . I heard he fell, bit his tongue, and eventually succumbed to gangrene."

"Hell of a way for a great man to die," William said, shaking his head.

As Clint had said, he'd respected Allan Pinkerton for everything he'd done with his life. But he wouldn't have gone so far as to call him a great man. He kept his opinion to himself, though.

"What's this got to do with Allan's death?"

"Everything," William said. "I've been contacted by someone who says he has information about my father's death."

"Information?"

"Proof," William said, "that he was murdered."

"And do they know who murdered him?"

"I don't know," William said. "What I've told you is all I have, except for one other thing."

"What's that?"

"They want to meet . . . in San Francisco."

"So go and meet them."

"I can't," William said.

"So send one of your men."

"My brother doesn't agree that we should commit company resources to this."

"What your brother doesn't know won't hurt him," Clint said.

"No," William said, "since our father died we've worked hand in hand to build this agency, to make it even bigger than our father did. I can't go behind his back."

"Wait a minute," Clint said. "You said he knew you were meeting me today?"

"Well . . . I may have lied about that."

"Then you're going behind his back to contact me."

"Well, yes . . . but I can't go behind his back to send one of our men to San Francisco."

"Or go yourself."

"Right."

"So you're asking me to go."

"Yes."

Clint stopped walking. William continued on for three steps before he stopped and turned.

"Why would I do that?" Clint asked.

"Why would you come here?" William asked. "All the way to Chicago to meet with some unknown someone? On the word of Jim West."

Clint stared at him.

"That's why you'll do this."

Clint stared at the man, then asked, "When's the meet?"

THREE

On the word of Jim West . . .

. . . Clint ended up in San Francisco, in a saloon that looked like it belonged on the Barbary Coast, not Market Street. The wooden floor was covered with sawdust. There were stuffed fish on the walls, along with nets and ropes and other fishing equipment.

Clint went to the bar and ordered a beer. It was surprisingly good.

"The owner a fisherman?" he asked.

"Used to be a sailor," the bartender said. "Gave up the sea and opened this place, but I think he must miss it."

"Looks like it."

"New in town?" the barkeep asked. He was tall, thin, in his fifties with some loose skin under his chin that jiggled when he talked.

"Just got in," Clint said. "Staying in a hotel down the street."

"Lookin' for anythin'?"

"Anythin'?"

"Girl," the man said, "two girls? An old lady, maybe? A boy?"

"No, thanks," Clint said. "I get my own women."

"Suit yerself."

Clint's instructions were to come to this saloon, have a beer at the bar, and wait to be approached. As with the walk in Washington Square Park, if no one approached him the first day, he was to come back.

Nobody came up to him the first day . . .

On the second day a girl approached him, but she was selling something—herself.

On day three he entered and walked to the bar. This was it for him. If no one came up to him, he was checking out of his hotel and into a place in Portsmouth Square to do some gambling. Just so the trip wouldn't be a total loss.

"Hey, buddy," the bartender said. "Back again? Beer?"

"Sure."

The beer was his only consolation. It was ice cold and very good.

"You wouldn't be lookin' for a game, wouldja?" the barman asked.

"What makes you think that?"

"Well, you ain't lookin' fer a girl," the man said. "I saw Lorie talkin' to ya yesterday, and ya didn't go with her."

"What if all I'm looking for is a beer?" Clint asked.

"Then ya wouldn't be comin' here for it," the bartender said. "There's plenty of other places in San Francisco to get beer."

"Yeah," Clint said, "but this is good beer."

"Well, yeah, you're right about that."

"What about the owner?" Clint asked. "Does he ever come around?"

"Few times a week," the bartender said.

"What's he do when he's not here?"

The bartender shrugged.

"I work for him, but we ain't friends," he said.

"Does he own any other places?"

"Dunno."

"What's his name?"

"Is that who yer lookin' fer?" the man asked. "You a debt collector?"

"Does he gamble?"

"Some."

"Well, I'm not looking to collect for anybody," Clint said. "I'll just have my beer and be on my way."

"Eddie MacDonald."

"What?"

"The owner," the bartender said. "His name's Eddie MacDonald."

"Don't know him," Clint said, "but thanks."

FOUR

There was a knock on the door of Clint's cheap hotel room. He'd been back from the saloon for a few hours and was thinking about getting some sleep so he could check out bright and early. He'd also need to send William Pinkerton a telegram telling him the meeting had not happened. Maybe whoever it was who had contacted Pinkerton had changed their mind.

He walked to the door with his gun held behind his back. When he opened it, two men showed him badges that said they were San Francisco police.

"I'm Inspector Burns; this is Inspector Logan," the older of the two said. "What's your name, sir?"

"What's this about?" Clint asked. "Are you going door to door?" He hadn't heard any knocking on any other doors.

"No, sir," Logan said, "we're lookin' for you."

"Me? You don't know my name, but you're looking for me?"

"Have you been drinkin' down the street at the Paradise Cove Saloon?"

"Is that what it's called?" Clint asked. "I never saw a sign."

"Apparently, it fell off," Burns said.

"Well, yes, I've been having a beer there the last two or three days."

"Why?" Burns asked.

"I was thirsty?"

"Sir, can we come in and talk?"

Clint wondered if he could let them in and get his gun holstered without them seeing.

"Can I have a minute to clean up?" Clint asked.

"That's okay," Burns said, moving past Clint, "we don't mind." Clint had to move because the older inspector was stocky. Logan, tall and thin with black hair, followed. Clint closed the door.

"Don't get nervous," he said. "I'm going to take my hand from behind my back."

He brought his hand out, holding his gun.

"You always answer the door holding your gun?" Burns asked, not looking nervous at all.

"Yes, I do."

"Where you from, sir?" Logan asked.

"Texas."

"You a rootin', tootin' cowboy?" Logan asked.

"I've never worked cows," Clint said. "You mind if I holster my gun?"

"Don't mind at all," Burns said.

Clint walked to the bedpost where the holster was hanging and returned the gun.

"I'm gonna ask you again, sir," Burns said. "Why'd you answer the door with your gun?"

"A man can't be too careful," Clint said.

"You got lots of enemies?" Logan asked.

"My fair share."

"That because you collect debts?" Burns asked.

"I don't collect," Clint said. "Who told you that? The bartender?"

"He might've mentioned it," Logan said.

"He said you weren't lookin' for a girl or a game. So he thought maybe you were lookin' for his boss."

"Well, I wasn't."

"But you asked about him?" Logan said. "Earlier this evenin'?"

"I was just makin' conversation."

"So you weren't interested in Eddie MacDonald?" Burns asked.

"No."

"What were you doin' drinkin' there?" Logan asked.

"They have good beer."

"Why are you stayin' here?" Burns said. "You don't look like you're doin' bad for money."

"Yeah," Logan said, "you can afford a better place to stay, can't ya? And a better place to drink?"

Both inspectors were looking the room over. Burns walked over to look at the gun.

"You mind?" he asked.

"No, go ahead."

Burns picked up the gun, looked at it, sniffed it. He looked at Logan and shook his head.

"It hasn't been fired," Clint said. "Who's been killed?"

"What makes you think somebody's been killed?" Logan asked.

"Your partner is sniffing my gun," Clint said. "You only do that to see if it's been fired."

"Eddie MacDonald," Burns said. "He was found shot to death in his office in back of the saloon."

"Sure you didn't know him?" Logan asked.

"Didn't know him; never saw him," Clint said.

Burns holstered the gun.

"You never told us your name, sir."

"No, I didn't," Clint said. "It's Clint Adams."

Logan looked disinterested, but Burns showed visible signs of recognizing the name.

"Clint . . . Adams?" he asked.

"That's right."

Burns looked at the gun again, then at Clint.

"What is it?" his partner asked.

"Holy Christ!" Burns said.

FIVE

Inspectors Burns and Logan asked Clint if he would accompany them to the police station. Clint, not wanting to get on the wrong side of the law, agreed.

They had a buggy out front, which fit all three of them snugly. They assured Clint that they would drive him back when they were done.

"If he's not in a cell," Logan added.

"He won't be," Burns said.

"I don't get it," Logan said to his partner. "Who is this guy?"

"You ain't up on your legends of the West, Logan?" Burns asked. "Clint Adams?"

"Yeah, he said that in his room," Logan said. "I still don't get it."

"Does the name 'the Gunsmith' ring a bell for you?" Burns asked.

"The Gunsmith?" Logan repeated. He jerked his thumb at Clint. "You mean . . . he's the Gunsmith?"

Burns looked at Clint.

"That's who you are, right?"

"Right."

Now Logan examined Clint from head to toe.

"He don't look like no legend to me," he said.

"Yeah, I know," Clint said. "You thought I'd be bigger. I get that a lot."

"It ain't about size, kid," Burns said.

Burns was sitting next to Clint, with Logan across from them. Logan leaned forward and lowered his voice, as if he thought Clint wouldn't be able to hear him.

"So why are we takin' him in if we're not gonna put him in a cell?"

"The boss is gonna want to question him."

"Your boss?" Clint asked. "Who would that be?"

"You wouldn't know him," Burns said. "Lieutenant Hargrove."

"You're right," Clint said. "I don't know him."

"But he's gonna know you," Burns said. "You can bet he's gonna know you."

"Why's that?"

"He's a student of the old West," Burns said. "Loves everythin' about it."

"That's why we're takin' him in?" Logan asked. "You show him off to the lieutenant?"

"I told you," Burns said, "the lieutenant is gonna want to question him."

Logan sat back and assumed a look of disgust.

When they got to the police station, Burns and Logan took Clint inside and walked him past a front desk and down a hallway. Clint had been in police stations before, in New York, Chicago, Denver, and San Francisco. This was not new to him.

They walked him to their boss's office. The door had the name Lieutenant David Hargrove on it. As they entered, the man behind the desk looked up. He was in his fifties, with very broad shoulders and a barrel chest. His receding hair was plastered down with hair gel that made his black hair gleam.

"What the hell is this?" he asked. "Burns? Who is this man?"

"Someone we're questioning about the MacDonald murder, Lieutenant."

"So why bring him here?"

"I thought you'd like to be part of the questioning."

"And why would I want to do that?"

"Maybe I should introduce the two of you," Burns suggested.

"My name's on the door, Burns," Hargrove said. "I suspect this gentleman can read."

"Well then," Burns said, "I guess I should just tell you his name. Lieutenant, this is Clint Adams."

The lieutenant hesitated, then looked Clint up and down, much the way Logan had done in the buggy.

"Adams?" the lieutenant repeated.

"Yes, sir."

"The Gunsmith?"

"That's right."

Hargrove looked at Clint again.

"How do you know?" the lieutenant asked.

"Sir?"

"How do you know this man is really Clint Adams?" Hargrove asked.

"Why would he lie about his name?" Burns asked. "There's no reason for it."

Hargrove looked at Clint.

"You're really the Gunsmith?"

"I really am," Clint said.

"Can you prove it?"

"If I have to."

"How?"

"I have some letters in my room," Clint said. "They're addressed to me."

"Anything else?"

"Well, what would you like me to do?" Clint asked. "Shoot something?"

Hargrove looked at Burns.

"Does he have a gun on him?" he asked. "Did you check him for a gun?"

"He left his gun and holster in his room, sir," Logan said.

"That doesn't mean he's not armed," Hargrove said. "Search him."

Burns turned to Clint.

"You mind?"

"Not at all."

Clint lifted his hand. Burns searched him, came up with the New Line in his belt behind his back.

"Jesus, Burns," the lieutenant said. "If he's not the Gunsmith—even if he is—he could have shot any one of us."

"Why'd you do this?" Burns asked.

"I'm not comfortable walking around unarmed," Clint said. "I'm too big a target."

"Let me see that," Hargrove said.

Burns handed him the gun. The lieutenant examined it.

"Colt New Line, right?"

"That's right," Clint said.

"I read something—" the lieutenant started, then stopped. He put the gun down on his desk. "Have a seat, Mr. Adams, this shouldn't take long. Inspectors, you can wait outside."

SIX

Lieutenant Hargrove sat back in his chair and regarded Clint, who was sitting directly opposite him.

"What are you doing in San Francisco, Mr. Adams?" he asked.

"I often come to San Francisco, Lieutenant," Clint said. "I like the city."

"What are you doing staying and drinking in that neighborhood?"

Clint shrugged.

"Just a change."

"Slumming?"

"I guess you could say that."

"You've been there . . . how long?"

"Three days."

"And I understand you've been drinking at the Paradise Cove all three days."

"It's walking distance from my hotel."

"And you've never met the owner?"

"Never. All my conversations have been with the bartender."

"Conversations about what?"

Clint shrugged.

"Whatever bartenders talk about."

Answering the policeman's questions were not hard. Clint was telling the truth. The only thing he was leaving out was the fact that he was waiting for someone to contact him.

"And you had no business with Eddie MacDonald?"

"I don't know Eddie MacDonald," Clint said. "Have never met him. And I'm willing to bet you don't have anyone who can say otherwise."

"No," Hargrove said, "At the moment we have no witnesses who can say that you and MacDonald knew each other."

"Or that I was even looking for him."

"The bartender said you and he talked about Eddie."

"I just asked who owned the saloon, out of curiosity," Clint said. "Like I said, the things you talk to a bartender about."

"Are you planning to stay in San Francisco for a few days more?"

"Actually, I was planning to leave tomorrow," Clint said.

"Well, I'd appreciate it if you didn't leave, just yet."

"How long do you want me to stay?"

"Unfortunately," Hargrove said, "until we find out who killed MacDonald."

"And I'm still a suspect?"

"I know who you are, Mr. Adams," Hargrove said. "I've read about you for years, and I've admired you. But yes, you're still a suspect."

"But I can go?"

"Yes," Hargrove said, "I'll have Burns and Logan take you back to your hotel. You'll be staying there?"

"No," Clint said, "I'll probably move to a hotel near or in Portsmouth Square."

"Now that's where I would've expected to find you, Mr. Adams. All right, if you'll just let me know what hotel you'll be moving to, you can go."

"I'll send word," Clint promised, "as soon as I get situated."

"Fine," Hargrove said. He stood up and offered his hand for the first time. "It was a pleasure to meet you, sir."

Clint stood up, shook the lieutenant's hand, and left his office.

SEVEN

The next morning Clint chose a hotel that was just off Portsmouth Square—far enough away that the action and the cost of the room were far less than what they were in the square. Yet this was miles beyond Market Street.

Clint had been coming to San Francisco for years, to stay, to gamble for a while. He knew a lot of the people who owned the saloons and halls and hotels. Most of them had since gone on to other things, some of them stayed, but he didn't like to always take advantage of the fact that they were his friends. So sometimes he came and stayed in a hotel where nobody knew him.

He got settled in his room, got himself a bath, then went out to hit some of the gaming palaces and saloons in Portsmouth Square.

But first he had to send a telegram.

His telegram to William Pinkerton in Chicago was short and sweet. "Three days," it said, "no contact. Sorry."

Clint departed the telegraph office on Kearny after

leaving the name of his hotel, the Diamond Palace, with the clerk in case of a reply. Eventually, he reached the Parker House, which was flanked by Samuel Dennison's Exchange and the El Dorado Gambling Saloon, owned by James McCabe and Thomas J. A. Chambers. He decided to spend some time moving from one to the other, having a drink, gambling a bit.

He was finding, as the day went by, that he was angrier and angrier with William Pinkerton for talking him into coming here. He had not met with the person he was supposed to meet, and he was mixed up in murder.

When Inspectors Burns and Logan had driven him back to his Market Street hotel, they had talked about the murder . . .

"Apparently," Burns had said, "somebody met with him in his office and strangled him."

"I would think I'd be a suspect if he'd been shot," Clint said.

"Shootin' him would've made noise," Logan said. "That saloon ain't usually crowded, but at least the bartender would've heard shots. Stranglin' was quieter."

"Who found him?" Clint asked.

"The bartender," Burns said. "Hadn't seen him all day, went back there after he closed up, and found him sittin' at his desk, dead."

"Maybe the bartender did it."

"That's one possibility we're lookin' into," Logan said.

"And are there others?"

"There's you," Logan said.

"I mean, besides me."

"Sure," Burns said. "Eddie wasn't a nice man. There are lots of people who might've wanted him dead."

"Sounds like it might take a while to solve his murder."

"What does it matter to you, if you didn't do it?" Logan asked.

"Your lieutenant told me not to leave town," Clint answered. "I think he wants me to stay around until you find the killer. Or, at least, until you clear me."

"Yeah," Logan said, nodding his head, "I guess that could take a long time."

"Or not," Burns added.

Clint figured he should be comfortable if he was going to have to stay in San Francisco indefinitely. But he also left word with the clerk of the Market Street hotel in case somebody was looking for him. And he knew he needed to send word to the police about where he was staying.

Whatever happened, whatever needed to be done, the Diamond Palace was going to be his base of operations.

He spent most of the first day in the Parker House and the Exchange. He didn't get to the El Dorado. He'd hit that the next day.

He went back to his hotel after midnight and stopped at the desk. The well-dressed young clerk was fresh and awake.

"Can I help you, sir?"

"I need to have a message hand delivered tomorrow morning."

"I can have that done for you. Do you have it written down?"

"Not yet."

The clerk pushed a pad of paper and a pencil at Clint.

"Thank you," Clint said. He wrote a note to Inspector

Burns, telling him where he was staying. He purposely
sent the note to the inspector, not the lieutenant. He folded
it, wrote Burns's name and the location of the police station on the back, then pushed it back to the clerk.

"There you go."

The clerk picked it up and said, "I'll have it delivered
first thing in the morning, sir."

"Thank you."

Clint took out two bits but the clerk waved his hand
and said, "Not necessary, sir. Just part of the Diamond
Palace service."

"Thank you."

"Sir?"

"Yes."

"Excuse me, but the owner of the hotel noticed your
name in our register?"

"And he wants to charge me double?"

The clerk gave Clint a small smile.

"She," the clerk said, "was wondering if you would
have breakfast with her tomorrow morning."

"Why is that?"

"She didn't tell me that, sir," the clerk said. "She just
told me to pass on the message."

"Well . . . don't know . . ."

"She did say she would forgo the cost of your first
two days' stay here."

Clint smiled.

"In that case, tell her I'll be glad to meet her at . . ."

"Eight a.m."

"Good," Clint said. "Eight a.m. it is."

EIGHT

The Diamond Palace was a smaller version of the Parker House, the Exchange, and the other hotels that were closer to Portsmouth Square. It did not have gambling, but it did have many of the hotel amenities the larger establishments had, and it also had a smaller version of their opulent dining rooms.

Clint came downstairs the next morning and saw the same clerk at the front desk. The man beckoned at him to come over to the desk.

"Sir, I just wanted you to know that your message has been hand delivered, as you requested."

"Thank you. Was there a response?"

"No, sir. Did you expect one?"

"No, that's fine," Clint said. "Thank you. Is your boss in the dining room?"

"Yes, sir. She has a regular table, every morning at eight."

"What's her name?"

"She is Mrs. Lillian Kingsforth, sir."

"Missus?"

"Yes, sir," the man said. "She is a widow."

"I see. Thanks."

"The maître d' will seat you."

"Thanks."

Clint walked to the entrance of the dining room and saw that the room was very full, most tables taken. A small, balding man in a tuxedo approached him.

"Sir?"

"My name is Clint Adams."

"Yes, sir. Follow me, please."

The man walked across the floor with an erect back and the carriage of a much larger man. Clint followed him to a table where a woman sat alone. As he approached, he appraised her. As she was seated, he judged that she'd probably be tall—five-eight or -nine—when she stood. As he got closer, he saw that she was older than she had looked from across the room, probably between forty and forty-five. She had a mane of fiery red hair, pale skin, wide, green eyes. When she saw the smaller man leading him to her table, she removed the cloth napkin from her lap, set it down on the table, and stood up. As he reached the table, he saw that she was even taller than he had predicted.

"Mr. Adams?"

"That's right."

"Thank you, Harmon," she said to the other man.

"Yes, Mrs. Kingsforth."

As the maître d' walked away, she looked at Clint and said, "My name is Lillian Kingsforth. Would you have a seat? I took the liberty of ordering steak and eggs for breakfast."

"That's fine, thank you," he said. He waited for her to reseat herself before seating himself.

"Coffee?" she asked.

"Yes, thanks."

She picked up the pot off the table and poured him a cup. From the smell he knew it would be strong enough for him. She apparently knew how he took his coffee and what he liked for breakfast. He didn't like being at a disadvantage, but he was willing to let her go at her own pace. After all, she was paying for the privilege.

As he tasted the coffee she asked, "Is it to your liking?"

"It's excellent." Not trail coffee, which was his favorite, but good. "I'm sure the breakfast will be the same."

"Yes, I'm very proud of my chef."

"Your clerk said you wanted to buy me breakfast and give me two complimentary nights in your hotel."

"That's right."

"But he didn't know why."

"No," she said, "I didn't tell him."

"But I assume you'll tell me?"

"Yes, I will," she said, "but why don't we talk about that after breakfast?"

"Okay," he said, "but while we're eating you'll have to tell me all about yourself."

"Maybe not all," she said, with a smile, "but a little."

NINE

"How was your breakfast?" Lillian Kingsforth asked.

"It was excellent, as promised," he said. "Now, as promised, I'd like to get to the point of your invitation. I'm curious."

During breakfast he found out that her husband was the owner of the hotel, had owned it for many years. She had married him when he was sixty and she was thirty. He had died at seventy, leaving the hotel to her. She had been the sole owner for four years, now.

"Very well," she said. "I have a problem—in fact, I have had this problem for some time now. It was only when I saw your name in the registration book—well, I thought you were the man to help me."

"With what?" he asked. "You're still being very vague."

"Are you in San Francisco on business or for pleasure, Mr. Adams?"

"A little of both, I suppose," he said. "I came here on business, but it didn't happen. So now I'm on to pleasure."

"So you're in no hurry to leave San Francisco?"

"No hurry," he said. He didn't bother telling her that he wasn't allowed to leave San Francisco, not for a while.

"Good," she said. "I'm under pressure to sell my hotel, Mr. Adams. I don't want to sell."

"Then don't."

"Well, when I said I was under pressure I meant that literally," she said. "I've been threatened. Some of my suppliers have refused to sell to me."

"How many times have you been threatened?"

The question seemed to surprise her.

"How many times would I need to be?" she asked. "I was threatened once, and then . . ."

"And then?"

"And then someone tried to kill me."

"How and when did that happen?"

"I was walking down the street and a crate fell from a window and almost hit me."

"There's no way that was an accident?"

"There was no reason for that crate to be near that window."

"I see."

"I think someone is going to try to kill me again."

"Have you gone to the police?"

"I don't have a good relationship with the law."

"Why is that?"

"I believe they suspect me of killing my husband."

"That's not unusual," Clint said. "I've run into that before."

"And?"

"And what?"

"When you ran into it before, did the woman kill her husband?"

"Yes," he said. "In fact, I think it was right here in San Francisco."

"Well, that's not the case this time," she said. "I didn't have to kill my husband. He managed to die all by himself."

"Leaving you this hotel."

"Yes."

"Is the hotel worth a lot of money?"

"Because of the proximity to Portsmouth Square," she said, "yes."

"And you've had offers to buy?"

"I believe I said I was being pressured to sell," she reminded him.

"Pressure from how many people?"

"One, I assume."

"And how many offers to buy have you had?"

"Several."

"So," Clint said, "you believe that the pressure, and the attempt, are coming from one of the people who made those offers."

"It seems logical."

"Why don't you hire a private detective, Mrs. Kingsforth?" he asked.

"I was going to," she said. "I've been looking for a reliable man, but when I saw your name in the registration book . . ." She shrugged.

"I'm not a detective," he said.

"You," she said, "are better. You are the Gunsmith."

"And you think having me in your employ will stop the pressures, and the attempts?"

"I hope so."

"But you can't employ me forever," he said. "Once I leave, they may very well start up again. What you need is someone to find out who is behind these attempts."

"I believe you're the man for that, too, Mr. Adams," she said. "And since you appear not to have anything else to do—but gamble, I assume—I'm willing to pay you well for your help."

"How well?"

She told him.

"That's very well," he said. He'd be able to gamble for quite a while on what she was offering him.

"And you can stay here indefinitely, for free," she added.

The offer was getting better and better, and he really didn't have anything better to do.

"All right."

"You'll do it?"

"I'll try to help," he said.

"That's wonderful," she said. "Shall I give you some money first—"

"I don't need any money yet," he said. "We'll save that for later. I'll take this excellent meal as a down payment."

"But that doesn't sound fair—"

"It's fine," he said. "Don't worry about it."

"Well . . . what do we do first?"

"I'll want a list of anyone who's made an offer to buy this place from you, anyone who's tried to pressure you, and then I'll want to see the place where the crate almost hit you."

"If we go to my office," she said, "I can give you a list now, and then we can walk to the place where the crate fell."

"Okay then," he said, standing up. "Let's go."

TEN

They walked from the dining room to her office, where she sat at her desk and wrote out a list from memory.

"Six names," she said, pushing the slip of paper across the desk to him. Five men, and one woman, but two of the men are partners, so it represents five offers."

"I get it," he said, pocketing the list. "How far is the site of the murder attempt?"

"A few blocks," she said. "I was walking down a side street toward a warehouse that we use."

"Did the crate fall from your building?"

"No, from another."

"Owned by who?"

"I don't know."

"We'll find out," he said. "Come on, let's go for a walk."

They walked together and he was under no illusion that the looks they were drawing were because of him. Lillian's red hair shone in the sunlight, and she was a tall, full-bodied woman. She matched his stride easily and walked with her chin up. She was quite a sight and he doubted anyone even saw him next to her.

"Here," she said, stopping in front of the building.

He looked up. It was two stories high, with large windows on the second floor. It wouldn't be hard to push a crate out one of them.

"Who was around when it fell?" he asked.

"There were some people on the street, but no one would admit to seeing anything."

"Did you see anyone when you looked up?"

"I was so frightened I didn't look up for a few moments. By that time if anyone had been there, they were gone."

"I can't blame you for that. All right, let's go back."

"You're not going in?"

"Not now," he said. "I'll come back and do it myself. I don't want you around when I do."

"I'm not frightened," she said, then added, "not now, anyway."

"I understand," he said, "but I'd still like to come back alone."

"All right," she said. "I have some work to do, anyway."

He took her arm, turned her, and they walked back.

When they got back to the hotel, she brought him into her office again and insisted on giving him some money.

"I'm sorry," she said, "but I'm a businesswoman. This is how I do business."

"Okay," he said and accepted a small down payment from her.

"What will your first move be?" she asked.

"Probably to have a drink and give my next move some thought," he said.

"But I thought—"

"I won't be reporting every move to you, Lillian," he said. "Let me see what kind of progress I can make and then we'll talk."

"Very well, Mr. Adams."

"And you'll have to call me Clint from now on."

"All right," she said. "My friends call me Lily."

"I'll talk to you soon, Lily," he said. "Just give me some time to start asking questions."

"Very well."

"And don't go for any walks."

"I can't just hide inside," she said. "I have a business to run."

"All right, but keep your excursions to a minimum," he said. "Do you have someone who can go with you?"

"Yes," she said. "I have Jesse."

"Jesse?"

"He's my . . . well, I don't want to say manservant. He was my husband's right hand and was left to me with the hotel."

"Is Jesse a capable man?"

"Yes, he's very capable."

"I'd like to meet him later," Clint said, "but for now, try to take Jesse with you wherever you go."

"All right," she said. "Perhaps you can meet him to-night?"

"That might be a good idea," Clint said. "Ask him to stop by my room."

"I'll do that."

"Good," Clint said. "For now I'm going to talk to

some people I know and see what I can find out about the people on your list."

As he left her office, she was opening a ledger book on her desk.

ELEVEN

Frank Ellington was a friend of Rick Hartman and had come to San Francisco two years before to put in a bid to buy the Faro House Saloon and Gaming Hall. Ellington had successfully made the buy, renamed the hall the House of Cards, and was now the owner of one of the most successful gaming establishments outside Portsmouth Square.

Clint had older friends in town, but he had the feeling that Ellington—fairly new in San Francisco compared to some of the other gambling barons—would have his finger on the pulse of the gaming community more firmly.

Clint walked to Kearny Street, where the House of Cards was located, and entered. If the building could have been moved ten feet, it would have been inside the square.

It was early, and only a few tables were in action. But as long as there were any gamblers on the floor, he knew the bar would be open.

"Help ya?" the bartender asked.

"Beer."

"Kinda early, ain't it?"

"What are you, the temperance police? I'm washing down a big breakfast."

"No need to get testy, friend," the bartender said. "You want a beer, then one beer comin' up."

The bartender drew a cold beer with a good head and set it down in front of Clint.

"Sorry," he said to the barman, "I'm kind of stuck here in town unwillingly. Didn't mean to take it out on you."

"No problem," the man said. "I'm a bartender. That's what I'm here for."

"Anyway," Clint said, "I'm looking for Frank."

"Frank?"

"Frank Ellington," Clint said. "Doesn't he own this place?"

"Oh, Mr. Ellington," the bartender said. "Sure. He has an office upstairs."

"Is he in there?"

"I don't know," the man said. "He pretty much comes and goes. Sometimes in and out the back door. The only time I know he's there is at night, when business is really booming."

"How can I find out if he's there?"

"Well, I wouldn't recommend going up and knocking on the door," the man said. "Unless you're a really good, old friend of his."

"I can't say I am," Clint said, "but I know someone who is."

"Well then, let's send him upstairs," the bartender suggested.

"Unfortunately, he's in Texas."

"Oh," the bartender said, "then I better send Kenny."

"Who's Kenny?"

"Kenny's the guy around here we'll all miss the least," the man said. "Who should Kenny say wants him?"

"Tell Kenny it's Clint Adams."

The bartender nodded, started away, then stopped short and looked at Clint.

"Adams?"

"That's right," Clint said. "Tell him I'm a friend of Rick Hartman."

"Rick Hartman," the bartender repeated, still looking at Clint funny. "I'll tell him."

The bartender went off to deliver the message. Clint had never met Ellington before, but had heard a lot about him from Rick Hartman. He had never heard that the man was a harsh boss or a man other men would be afraid of.

He drank his beer and waited.

TWELVE

Frank Ellington held the girl's head in his hands lovingly as she continued to suck on him. This was one of the little pleasures of running his own place, interviewing the girls who wanted jobs in the House of Cards. All they had to do was satisfy him, and they got hired.

This one was very good. A little brunette with a bee-stung mouth you never would have thought could accommodate the entire length and width of his penis. Ellington was a well-endowed man, which is why he had chosen this particular test for the women. If they could please him, they'd be able to please anyone.

The girl's head bobbed up and down on him. His cock, glistening with her saliva, slid in and out of her mouth and, occasionally, bumped the back of her throat so that she gagged.

When the knock came at his door he was immediately livid.

"What the hell—" he roared.

"Sorry, Mr. Ellington," Kenny's voice said, timidly, "but there's a man downstairs to see you."

"Who the hell is it?"

"He says he's a friend of Rick Hartman," Kenny said. "His name's Clint Adams."

He looked down at the girl, felt himself nearing climax.

"Tell him I'll be down in five minutes."

"Yes, sir."

He looked down at the girl again, and she was looking up at him, her little tongue tickling the spongy head of his cock.

"You've got five minutes to get this job," he told her.

She practically swallowed him then, going back to work in earnest.

Six minutes later Ellington came down the stairs and entered the saloon through a doorway behind the bar. The girl had gotten the job.

"Here he is," the bartender said. "Hey, Boss, this is Clint—"

"Clint Adams," Ellington said, sticking out his hand. "Go back to what you were doin', Wesley. How are ya, Adams?"

Ellington was a big man gone to fat but still had a lot of strength in his grip. If he was the same man Rick Hartman had spoken of many times, he had gained about forty or fifty pounds since Rick last saw him.

"I'm doing okay."

"What are you doing in San Francisco?"

"If we can go somewhere we can talk," Clint said, "I'll tell you."

"Sure," Ellington said, figuring the girl was gone by now. "Let's go upstairs."

Before they left, though, he said to the bartender,

"Damn it, two beers over here, Wesley. What the hell are ya doin'?"

"You told me to go back—"

"Never mind what I told you, gimme what I want!" Ellington shouted.

"Yes, sir."

The bartender put two beers on the bar top. Ellington picked them both up.

"Follow me."

He led Clint through the doorway behind the bar and up a flight of stairs. They went through a door into a large office with the biggest desk Clint had ever seen. Ellington put one beer down on the desk, then walked around it and sat down.

"Have a seat," he said. "Let's talk. How's Rick?"

"Rick's fine," Clint said, picking up the beer. "If he knew I was here, I'm sure he would have sent his regards."

"And why are you here?"

"As it turns out," Clint said, "I'm here for a very different reason than the one that originally brought me here."

"What was that?"

"That's not important," Clint said. "I'm doing something else, now. It involves these people." He placed the list Lily had given him on the desk and pushed it to Ellington's side of the desk.

Ellington picked it up and read it.

"You know any of those people?" Clint asked.

"I know all of these people," Ellington said. "What's your interest in them?"

"I want to know which of them wants a woman named Lillian Kingsforth dead."

"Ah, the lovely Lily Kingsforth," Ellington said, putting the list down. "I heard some of these people were trying to buy her out, but I hadn't heard that anyone tried to kill her."

"I need to know as much as I can about these people," Clint said, picking the list up again. "Can you help me with that?"

"Sure," Ellington said. "How soon do you want the information?"

"As soon as possible."

Ellington nodded.

"Come back here this evening and I'll have it for you."

"That soon?"

"I just need to get it all written down," Ellington said.

"By this evening?"

"Come back at nine," Ellington said. "Have some drinks, do some gambling. I'll let you know when it's ready."

"Should I leave the list?" Clint asked, standing up.

"No," Ellington said. "I'll remember."

"Okay," Clint said, "thanks."

"Don't mention it," Ellington said. "Any friend of Rick's . . ."

Ellington walked Clint back down to the saloon.

"Another beer?"

"No, thanks," Clint said. "I've had enough for now."

"I assume you're staying with the lady?" Ellington asked. "I mean, at her hotel?"

"That's right."

"If I find out anything urgent I'll send word," the other man said.

"Thanks, Ellington."

"Just call me Frank, Clint."

As Clint left, Ellington was berating the bartender about something. Clint hoped there was enough left of the man Rick Hartman used to know to get the job done for him.

THIRTEEN

When Clint got back to the Diamond Palace, there was a message at the front desk for him. Clint read it right there and then. It said: "Meet me at seven p.m. tonight, outside the Alhambra." It wasn't signed.

"How did this get here?" he asked the clerk.

"I found it on the desk, sir."

"How did it get on your desk without you seeing someone put it there?"

"Honest, sir, I was only away from the desk for a minute," the clerk said. "I could get fired if you—"

"Forget it," Clint said. "Just keep a sharp eye out from now on. I want to know if any strangers are hanging around."

"Strangers?"

"Anybody you don't recognize. Understand?"

"Yes, sir."

Clint put the note in his pocket and went up to his room. Whoever had sent the message had picked one of the busiest places in Portsmouth Square to meet, and he was sure it was no accident.

He went to his window and stared out at the street below. There wasn't much for him to do until seven, when he would keep his meeting despite not knowing who it was with, and then nine, when he was to go back to the House of Cards.

The meeting, he was sure, was going to be about William Pinkerton's business. There was no one else who would send him that kind of note. No one except for Ellington knew that he was working for Lily Kingsforth, so the meet had to be about his original business. Someone had probably gone to the Market Street hotel looking for him and been directed to the Diamond Palace by the clerk there.

Suddenly, he remembered the telegram he'd sent to Pinkerton in Chicago. Apparently, there had been no response from William, yet. That didn't sit right with him. He had been sure the man would send back a reply as soon as he read Clint's telegram.

He went back down to the front desk. Not only did he want to check on the telegram but he also decided to check on that building Lily had walked him to, the one the crate had fallen from.

"I haven't seen anyone yet, sir," the clerk said, hurriedly.

"That's okay," Clint said. "I wouldn't expect you to this soon. I just wanted to ask if a telegram came for me?"

"No, sir," the clerk said. "I would have given it to you as soon as you came in, sir."

"Okay, look, if a telegram does come for me while I'm out, I want you to put it in my room. Better yet, just slip it under the door so it's there when I get back."

"Yes, sir," the clerk said. "You can count on me, Mr. Adams, sir."

"I know I can."

"And sir?"

"Yes?"

"Uh, thank you for not telling Mrs. Kingsforth about me, uh, being away from the desk—"

"That'll be our little secret, okay?"

"Yes, sir."

"And we won't mention it again, right?"

"Right, sir," the clerk said. "My lips are sealed."

"Okay," Clint said. "I'll be back in a little while."

"I'll be on the lookout, sir," the clerk said, "for everything."

FOURTEEN

Clint retraced his steps from that afternoon, when Lily took him to the building. It was a large two-story warehouse, with several doors, all of which were locked. He knocked on all of them, banged on them, but nobody answered. There was a hardware store across the street, so he went over there.

He entered and waited for the man behind the desk to finish with a customer.

"Can I help ya?" the man asked.

"I'm interested in that building across the street," Clint said.

"Interested?"

"Do you know who owns it?"

"No, I don't."

"Do you see people going in and out?"

"Well, sure, sometimes."

"A while ago a crate fell from a window, almost hit a woman. You know anything about that?"

"What would I know?"

"Well, for instance, did you even know that it happened?"

"Well, sure, I was here, I heard the crash, but I didn't see no woman."

"From here?" Clint turned, to see what he could see out the window from where he was standing.

"Well, no," the man said. "I walked to the door and looked out."

"And you didn't see a woman who was almost hit by the crate?"

"No."

"And after the crate hit the ground did anyone come out of the building?"

"No, not that I saw, and I stood there a few minutes," the man said.

"So a crate fell and nobody did anything about it?"

"Well, they musta, 'cause when I went home it was gone."

"And did the police come?"

"If they did, they didn't talk to me," the clerk said, "and I never saw them."

"That's strange."

"Sure is," the man said. "I got storage on my second floor, and if somethin' fell outta my window, the police would be on me right away, I can tell you that!"

"Okay," Clint said, "thanks."

"You gonna try to get inside that building?" the man asked.

"I think so."

"Should be interestin'," the clerk said. "I ain't never even seen any of their doors open. I always wondered who owned it."

"If I find out," Clint said, "I'll let you know."

* * *

Back across the street Clint again pounded on the door, but no one answered. He tried to see inside some windows, but they were apparently blocked from the inside. He backed up and just about stepped into the path of a passing buckboard in an attempt to see some of the upper window. For a moment he thought he saw someone looking out one of them, but he couldn't be sure.

He decided this was something else Frank Ellington could help him with, finding out who owned this building and what was inside.

He turned and headed back toward his hotel.

Across the street the hardware store clerk watched as Clint pounded on doors and tried to see through windows, then gave up and left.

The clerk looked up and was sure he saw someone looking out one of the second-floor windows.

Harry Dean heard the pounding on the door the first time and ignored it. Those were his instructions. Ignore any knocking at the door, and never open them. He had also been told never to go to the windows, but when the pounding started again his curiosity got the better of him. He left his station at a small desk and walked to the front windows, which—for the most part—had been painted over, although from outside it just looked like they were covered with dirt.

He looked down at the street and, as a man backed into the street and looked up, he suddenly jerked back, hoping he hadn't been seen.

As the man on the street walked away, Harry chanced another look. This time, though, he also looked across

the street and saw the clerk standing in the doorway of
the hardware store. For a split second he thought they
locked eyes, but then he pulled back again and stayed
away from the window after that.

FIFTEEN

When Clint got back to the Diamond House, he went to his room to rest. At quarter to seven he went back down, and the desk clerk waved him over.

"You got something for me?" he asked.

"No, sir, but Mrs. Kingsforth would like you to go to her office."

"When?"

"Now. Do you remember the way, sir?"

"I do. Thanks."

Clint went down the hall to Lily's door and knocked.

"Come in," her voice said.

He opened the door and entered. Immediately, his arms were pinned behind his back by someone whose strength was immense. He tried hard, but couldn't break free.

"Jesse, let him go!" Lily said. "That's Mr. Adams."

Clint's arms were freed, and Jesse turned him around. He had to look up to see the man's smile.

"Sorry," Jesse said. "Can't be too careful."

"Clint, this is Jesse, the man I told you about," Lily said. "Jesse, Clint Adams."

"Glad to meet ya," Jesse said, sticking out a hand the size of a ham. He was six and a half feet tall, almost that wide, dark-haired, about forty.

"Lily," Clint said, "with Jesse around to protect you why do you need me?"

"Don't get me wrong," she said. "I feel safe with Jesse around, but he doesn't carry a gun, and he's not a detective."

"No gun?" Clint asked, looking at Jesse.

"I'd just shoot myself in the foot," Jesse said.

"I see." Clint turned to Lily. "I'm not a detective, either."

"I think I should keep Jesse around me while you find out who's behind all of this," she said. "The pressure, the attempt on my life."

"Yes, about that," Clint said. "I talked to somebody across the street from that building. He heard the crate fall, saw it, but didn't see you."

"Well, as soon as it hit the ground I got away from there as fast as I could. I was hoping no one saw me."

"Looks like you got your wish," Clint said.

"Have you found out anything else?"

"No," Clint said, "not yet, but I'm working on those names you gave me."

"Well, I just wanted you to meet Jesse," she said. "If you need him for anything, he'll be available."

"Be my pleasure to help, Mr. Adams," Jesse said, still smiling.

"I'll keep that in mind, Jesse," Clint said. "I have an appointment at seven, and it looks like I'm going to be late. We'll talk again, soon."

"Yes," Lily said, "soon."

"Jesse," Clint said, with a nod, and left the office.

* * *

Clint left the hotel and walked toward Portsmouth Square. As he was approaching the Alhambra, he saw a crowd assembled out in front. He moved to the fringe of the crowd and asked somebody, "What's going on?"

"Some man got run down by a buckboard," a man answered.

"Is he dead?" Clint asked.

"Dead as can be," the man said.

"Anybody know who he is?"

The man shrugged and said, "Can't see a thing from back here."

Well, he was right about that.

Clint started pushing through the crowd until he got near the front. From there he could see the mangled body of a man lying in the street. He was obviously dead. There was one policeman standing near the body, while another tried to hold back the crowd.

"Anybody call for a doctor?" he asked.

"Doctor's on the way," the policeman said, "and more police."

"More police," Clint said. "That's good."

"Do you know this man, sir?" the policeman asked.

"No," Clint said, "I don't know him, at all."

But he had the uncomfortable feeling that this was the man he was supposed to be meeting. If he hadn't been about ten minutes late, maybe he would have.

"Do you know his name?" Clint asked.

"Why would you be interested in his name," the policeman asked, "if you don't know him?"

"Well," Clint said, "I really can't tell all that much from what I can see, but if you told me his name—"

"We don't know his name yet, sir," the young policeman admitted. "We're waiting for a superior officer to come."

"I see."

"If you like," the man said, "you can wait and talk with Lieutenant Hargrove when he gets here."

"Lieutenant Hargrove?"

"Yes," the man said, "he's going to come with Inspectors Burns and Logan. At least, that's what we were told."

SIXTEEN

In the end Clint decided to stay around, even though it might create trouble for him. He wanted to at least find out the dead man's name. Maybe if he could find out what he was doing there, he'd know whether or not it was the man he was supposed to meet.

So he waited . . .

Inspectors Burns and Logan finally appeared, with Lieutenant Hargrove behind them. There were also several other uniformed policemen who set about helping the other man hold back the crowd.

"What happened?" Burns asked the two policemen.

"Not sure," the first policeman said. "Witnesses said a buckboard ran this guy down."

"That sounds like it was accidental," Hargrove said. "Why are we here?"

"Witnesses also said it was done deliberately."

"Great," Logan said, "now we're gonna have to question everybody."

"Including me," Clint said, loudly.

The two inspectors and the lieutenant looked over at Clint.

"Adams?" Burns asked. "What are you doin' here?"

"I was in the area, saw the commotion," Clint said.

"Let him through," Hargrove said.

The policeman let Clint pass, and he joined the others, looking down at the body.

"Did you see this happen?" Hargrove asked.

"No," Clint said, "I only saw the crowd."

"Do you know him?" Burns asked.

"I'm not sure," Clint said. "I haven't gotten a clear look at him."

"Okay, well, take one," Logan said. He leaned down and rolled the dead man over so they could all see his face. "Know 'im?"

Clint leaned over, took a clear look at the man's face, and determined that he'd never seen him before.

"No," he said, "I don't know him."

"Anybody know this man?" Burns shouted to the crowd of onlookers.

If anyone did, they did not speak up.

"All right," Hargrove said, "we'll have to get him out of the street. I'm going into the Alhambra. I'm gonna get a room from them for us to use in questioning people. Just get us some witnesses to talk to. Somebody must have seen something." Hargrove turned to Clint. "Adams, you come with me. I want to question you, first."

"Why?" Clint asked. "I told you, I got here after the fact."

"The fact that you're here at all interests me," Hargrove said. "I'm not going to take your gun or strongarm you, but I'd like you to come with me . . . please."

"Okay," Clint said, "since you put it that way."

Hargrove turned to Burns and Logan and said, "I'll see you men inside."

"Yes, sir," Burns said.

"Adams?"

Inside the Alhambra, Hargrove got nothing but cooperation. Any gambling hall in San Francisco wants no trouble from the law, so pretty much any building he'd have gone into would have given him a room. Rather than a hotel room, though, the Alhambra gave him one of the back rooms that was used for private poker games. Eventually, he and Clint were seated at a green felt–covered table with cups of coffee in front of them.

"What's been happening to you since I last saw you?" Hargrove asked.

"Not much," Clint said. "I sent word to you that I was staying at the Diamond House."

"Yes, you did," the lieutenant said, "and I appreciate that. Have you made any progress with the business that brought you to town?"

"No."

"And this man?" Hargrove asked. "Would he have had anything to do with that?"

"To tell you the truth, Lieutenant," Clint said, "I don't know. As I told you, I don't know him, never saw him before, and certainly never spoke to him."

"Uh-huh."

The lieutenant gave Clint a dubious look, so he decided to try to change the subject.

"What about your case?" Clint asked. "Any progress on who murdered that saloon owner?"

"No, none," Hargrove said. "I've got Burns and Logan working on it."

As if on cue both inspectors appeared at the door.

"We've got a few witnesses out here, Lieutenant," Burns said.

"Good," Hargrove said, "bring them in one at a time. That'll be all, Adams. Thanks for the cooperation."

"Sure."

Clint got up and walked out. Just outside the door there was a line of about a half a dozen people, mostly men.

Before leaving he turned to Burns.

"What was the dead man's name?"

"We found a wallet on him," Burns said. "Apparently belonged to a man named Walter Trench. Do you know that name?"

Clint shook his head.

"I never heard of him."

"Well, that's who this was, unless he stole that wallet."

"That's a possibility," Logan chimed in. "We got lots of pickpockets working Portsmouth Square."

"A pickpocket would have more than one wallet on him," Burns said.

"Unless this was the first of the day for him," Logan argued.

Clint decided to leave the Alhambra and let the two inspectors argue the point without him. He'd never heard of the man, and that was all he cared about.

He had another stop to make and now he was going to be late for that one, too.

SEVENTEEN

When Clint entered the House of Cards, the topic of discussion in the crowded hall was the dead man in the street. He listened to several conversations, but no one knew anything. They were just rehashing what everyone had seen or heard from the police.

Clint went to the bar and ordered a beer.

"Hey, you came back," Wesley said.

"Got an appointment with your boss."

"Oh."

"I'll have a beer."

Wesley went off and came back with a full mug.

"You don't like Ellington very much, do you?" Clint asked.

Wesley looked nervous. "Are you friends with him?"

"No," Clint said. "I told you this afternoon, friend of a friend. But to tell you the truth, I'm not seeing the same man my friend told me about."

The bartender leaned on the bar. There was a lot of conversation going on around them. He lowered his voice and Clint had to strain to hear.

"He ain't the same man who hired me," Wesley said.

"How's that?"

"I came walkin' in here when the place was empty, wasn't even open yet. He was excited, you know? Said this place was his dream. We talked about my experience and he hired me. I was the first person he hired. He said we were gonna build this place together."

"You were going to be his partner?"

"No, that ain't what he meant," Wesley said. "He just meant when he hired the rest of his staff we'd all work together. And he said he'd be treatin' everybody fair."

"And he hasn't?"

Wesley wet his lips. "He treats everybody like crap," he said. "And he makes . . ."

"Makes what?"

"He makes the girls have sex with him, as part of their . . . job interview. If they do it, they get the job."

"And after they have the job?"

"Well, if they wanna keep their job . . ."

"I see."

"Which doesn't mean he can't help you with your problem," Wesley said, "but . . ."

"I should watch my back."

"Yeah," the bartender said. "I mean, he's gonna want somethin' back, eventually."

"Well," Clint said, "unfortunately, that does sound fair."

Wesley shrugged, leaned back. "You asked."

"Yes, I did," Clint said. "Thanks for the answer, Wesley."

"Mr. Adams?"

Clint turned and saw the young man named Kenny standing behind him.

"Yes?"

"Mr. Ellington says I should bring you to his office now."

"Okay," Clint said, "lead the way."

"Yes, sir," Kenny said. "This way."

"Can I take my beer?"

"Oh, yeah," Kenny said, "Mr. Ellington said to bring him one."

"Wesley?" Clint called. "A beer for Mr. Ellington."

EIGHTEEN

"Ah, that's what I've been waiting for," Frank Ellington said as Clint and Kenny entered, Kenny carrying Ellington's beer. "Put it on the desk and get out, Kenny."

"Yes, sir."

Kenny put the beer mug on the desk for his boss and quickly left. Clint sat in the chair he'd occupied earlier in the day.

"A lot of activity on the street," he said.

"So I heard." Ellington lifted his beer and drank half of it. "Ahhh! Well, I got that information you wanted." He pushed a piece of paper over to Clint. "There are the addresses where you can find all those people."

"I was hoping for more than just addresses," Clint said.

"Like what?"

"Impressions," Clint said. "What you think of them. How likely you think they are to kill to get what they want."

"All that?"

"All that."

Ellington sat back in his chair.

"We can do that now. Fire away."

Clint wondered why they hadn't just done this earlier, but he decided to let Ellington do it his way, as long as he got the information.

Clint looked at the list. He had given Ellington six names representing five offers to buy. The list in front of him had four names on it, representing three offers.

"Yes, you'll notice two names missing," Ellington said. "That's because one of them is dead, and the other has left San Francisco."

"Recently?"

"Very recently," Ellington said, "which is probably why the lovely Lily didn't even know about it."

"I'll check in with her," Clint said. "All right, what can you tell me about Adrian Webster?"

"Came here five years ago from England. He now owns two hotel and gaming halls, neither of which is as near Portsmouth Square as the Diamond House."

"If he has two gaming halls, why does he want the Diamond House?" Clint asked. "It's a hotel with no saloon or gambling."

"Yes, but the building is large enough to put in a saloon and gaming hall. The lovely Lily has no interest, so a lot of that space is going to waste."

"Does he represent any interests other than his own?" Clint asked.

"Partners, you mean? No, Mr. Webster is an independent operator, much like myself."

"What about Peter Forrest?"

"Now, he's a different story. He does not own any properties himself other than the Lucky Lady Gambling Hall, and he does represent other interests. That's his business. He brokers deals and takes a percentage. He does quite well for himself."

"Would either of these men kill for a deal?"

Ellington laughed. "Either of those men would kill their mothers for a deal."

"I see. And these two? Lily told me these two men were partners?"

"She's partially right."

"How do you mean?"

"Harold and Chris Garvin are partners, all right," Ellington said, "but Chris is a woman, not a man."

Clint frowned.

"I don't see Lily making that mistake."

"Unless," Ellington said, "she only met the male half of the partnership."

"Is that likely?"

"Not only likely, but probable," Ellington said. "Harold usually handles face-to-face meetings, while Chris handles the finances."

"And do they own any properties now?"

"Several, all over town," Ellington said, "including Portsmouth Square and the Barbary Coast."

"The Barbary Coast?"

"Very profitable area," Ellington said.

"Yeah, if you're involved with shanghaiing sailors," Clint said.

"That still goes on, sure, but there are hotels and gaming halls going up there. Believe me, it's a gold mine. I'm trying to buy some property down there, myself."

"Hmm, things have changed while I've been away from San Francisco."

"Can I help you with anything else?" Ellington asked.

"I think I've imposed on you enough, Mr. Ellington."

"That's Frank to you, Clint," Ellington said, as they both stood. "Remember that. And come back if you do think of something else I can do."

"I'll do that."

The two men shook hands and Clint left, taking his beer mug with him.

NINETEEN

Clint was in his room trying to read but not doing a very good job of it. He decided that, come morning, he'd send a telegram to William Pinkerton in Chicago and ask him if he knew a man named Walter Trench. If Trench wasn't the man he was supposed to meet, then the right man had gotten lost in the crowd. If he wasn't the man, then his death had coincidentally taken place in front of the Alhambra, where Clint was supposed to have his meeting and Clint still—after all these years—did not like coincidence.

He was still trying to read the Dickens novel he'd recently started when there was a knock on the door. He put the book down, plucked his gun from his hanging holster, and walked to the door.

"Who is it?"

"We were supposed to meet earlier," a low, hoarse voice said.

"Where?"

"Front of the Alhambra."

He opened the door, holding his gun behind it, at the ready. He was surprised to see a woman standing in the hall.

"Hurry. Let me in," she said in a deep voice.

Clint hesitated a second, but when the woman showed him her empty hands he opened the door wider and let her in.

"Glad to see you're careful," she said, noticing the gun in his hand.

"Were you there?" he asked. "In the crowd?"

"Yes," she said. "You got anything to drink?"

"I have a small bottle of whiskey, in the top dresser drawer."

She rushed to the dresser, got the bottle, opened it, and took a deep drink. Her full lips glistened with whiskey until she wiped it away with the back of her hand. She was tall, wearing trail clothes that were too big for her—not too short, but too large for her slender frame.

She put the bottle back in the dresser drawer, but left it open.

"Did you know the dead man? Walter Trench?" Clint asked, holstering his gun. "Did he have anything to do with this?"

"Walter," she said, nodding, crossing her arms as if she were cold. "He was my partner."

"Partner?"

"We're both Pinkertons."

"Ah."

"He was supposed to meet you; I was supposed to cover your backs."

"What happened?"

"That buckboard came out of nowhere," she said. "I couldn't believe it when it ran Walter down." She was looking down as she spoke. Now she looked up at him. "Why were you late?"

"I'm sorry," he said. "I . . . got held up earlier, it put me behind all day."

She turned, fished the bottle from the drawer, and took another drink, then set it on top of the dresser, this time.

"So Walter Trench was going to tell me something about Allan Pinkerton's death?"

"What? No, Walter didn't know anything. Neither did I. You were supposed to meet with someone when you first got here, weren't you?"

"I was, but he never showed up," Clint said, "and I got involved with another killing."

"Who?"

"A saloon owner named Eddie MacDonald. Do you know him?"

"Heard of him, but I didn't know him."

"Did your partner?"

"I don't think so. Was he the one who was going to tell you—"

"I don't know," Clint said. "I never got to talk to him."

"Well, if you never met with anybody, what have you been doin'?"

"I sent your boss a telegram telling him I was moving to this hotel, and I left my new location at that Market Street hotel. If anyone wanted to find me, they could."

"And no one has?"

"You and your partner," Clint said. "And, by the way, why?"

"We got a telegram from our boss telling us to check in with you."

"Why?"

"I don't know. To find out what you were doin', I guess," she said, with a shrug. "It was Walter who read the telegram."

"You didn't see it?"

"No," she said. "Walter was the senior operative."

"How long have you been a Pinkerton?"

"Almost a year."

She reached for the whiskey again, but he crossed the room and plucked it from her hand.

"That's enough of that," he said. He capped it and put it away. "You need to stay sober and alert."

"Why?" she asked. "I don't know what to do. Walter was in charge."

"Well, Walter's gone and now you're in charge," Clint said.

She gave him a resentful look and he wondered if Walter Trench was more to her than the senior operative.

"You've got to get yourself together," Clint said. "From the way you're dressed I assume you're undercover."

"Well, I don't dress like this normally," she said.

"So you have someplace to stay?"

"A flophouse on the Barbary Coast."

"I heard that was getting better."

"Not where we're stayin'," she said.

"Okay, I suppose you better go back there," he said. "Contact your boss in the morning for instructions."

"Should I talk to the police?" she asked. "Tell them who Walter was?"

"Like I said, check with your boss."

"Well, aren't you the senior operative now?" she asked.

"You haven't told me your name."

"It's Kat," she said. "Katherine Crawford, but everybody just calls me Kat."

"Kat, I'm not an operative. I don't work for Pinkerton."

"Then what are you doin' here?"

"Asking myself the same question."

"Huh?"

"I'm just doing William and Robert a favor."

"You know them?"

"Yes, I do."

"And did you know their father?"

"I knew Allan, yeah."

"What was he like?"

"He was an annoying son of a bitch."

She looked surprised.

"A brilliant man," he added, "but an annoying son of a bitch."

TWENTY

Clint got Kat to leave and go back to her hotel. She agreed she would send a telegram to William Pinkerton in the morning and would let Clint know what the reply was. They were going to meet near her hotel on the Barbary Coast.

Meanwhile, Clint would leave himself available to still be contacted while at the same time working on Lily Kingsforth's troubles.

The next morning after breakfast Clint started on Lily's problem. The first of the names he was going to talk to were Harold and Chris Garvin.

Clint wanted to take a look at the Barbary Coast. It had been a while since he'd been there. He took a cab to a hotel that was owned by the Garvins. The Coast Hotel was nothing like the buildings in Portsmouth Square but it was far better than anything he'd ever seen on the Barbary Coast in past years.

Clint entered the hotel lobby and walked to the front desk.

"Yes, sir?" a nattily dressed young clerk asked.

"I'm looking for Harold or Chris Garvin."

"The owners?"

"That's right," Clint said. "They are the owners, aren't they?"

"Oh, yes, sir."

"Are they here?"

"I believe Mrs. Garvin is in the office," the clerk said. "I'm not sure if Mr. Garvin is in the building."

"Well then, I'll settle for Mrs. Garvin."

"Uh, well, Mrs. Garvin rarely sees anyone, sir. Mr. Garvin usually—"

"But Mr. Garvin isn't here," Clint said. "Would you please tell Mrs. Garvin I'd like to see her?"

"Well, yes, sir, but I can't promise—"

"Just tell her."

"Yes, well . . . what is your name?"

"Clint Adams."

There was no hint of recognition on the young man's face.

"If you'll wait here, I will tell her."

"I'll be right here," Clint promised.

"Yes, well . . ." the clerk said and went through a curtained doorway behind him.

Clint waited five minutes and then the young man returned, with a surprised look on his face.

"Will you come with me?" he asked. "Mrs. Garvin will see you."

"Thank you."

Clint followed the man down a hallway to an open door, where he stopped and stepped aside.

"Inside, sir."

"Thanks," Clint said again.

Clint entered the room and saw a beautiful woman in

her thirties standing behind a desk. Just standing there she took his breath away. She was as tall as Lily Kingsforth, but blonde where Lily was red-haired. She had big, wide blue eyes and a luscious mouth, with an upper lip as full as her lower. She was also about ten years younger than Lily.

"Mr. Adams?" she asked. "I'm Christine Garvin."

Clint found himself at a loss for a moment, then regained his voice.

"I'm, uh, very pleased to meet you."

"I understood you wanted to talk to my husband?" she said.

"Or you," Clint said. "Either, or both."

"Well, my husband usually deals with . . . people, but since we're here why don't you have a seat and tell me what I can do for the Gunsmith?"

TWENTY-ONE

"Do you know Lily Kingsforth?" Clint asked, taking a seat.

"Lillian Kingsforth?" Christine asked. "The owner of the Diamond Palace? Yes, we know her."

"You tried to buy her place."

"We made an offer," Christine said. "She turned us down."

"How did you take that?"

"Me?" Christine shrugged. "We have other properties."

"And how did your husband take it?"

"Harold? He takes things a little harder than I do. He doesn't like to be turned down."

"And how mad does he actually get?"

"Well, mad . . . that's a strong word."

"Angry, then. Disappointed. Would his feelings be strong enough to want to . . . kill?"

"Kill? Kill who?"

"Lily."

"Are you crazy?" she asked, laughing. "We don't kill people if they don't sell to us."

"Do you apply pressure?"

"Of course not."

"And what about Adrian Webster and Peter Forrest?"

"What about them?"

"Do you know them?"

"Of course," she said. "They're in business, we're in business. We know them."

"They have also tried to buy the Diamond House," Clint said. "Why are so many people interested in that place?"

"It's a prime piece of property," she said.

"Why?"

"I'm not really sure," she said, "but that's what Harold says."

"Where is your husband, Mrs. Garvin?"

"He's out."

"Out where?"

"On business," she said. "He'll be back later. I believe he's at one of our other properties."

"And you," Clint asked, "you never go out?"

"Oh, I go out," she said, "I just don't go out on business. My husband handles all the, uh, meetings."

"Why is that?"

"Oh," she said, "I'm not very good at them. Would you like a drink?"

"Why not?"

She went to a sideboard and came back with two glasses of sherry. She was wearing an expressive dress that was cinched at the waist, accentuating her full bosom. She was as tall but not as slender as he had figured while she was seated.

"Seems to me you do pretty well as a hostess," he said to her as she handed him the glass.

She planted her butt on her desk and looked down at him.

"Oh, I'm a good hostess," she said, "it's business meetings I'm bad at."

"Why is that?"

"I have no patience with idiots," she said, "and it seems to me that's all you deal with in business meetings. So I leave them to my husband."

"Is that wise?"

"What do you mean?"

"Does your husband tell you everything that goes on at a meeting?"

"Why wouldn't he?"

"Well," Clint said, "he might only tell you what he thinks you need to know."

She stood up and walked back around her desk. It seemed like she didn't like where the conversation was going.

"What's the difference?"

"Well," Clint said, "if you trust him, I guess there is no difference."

"Why wouldn't I trust him?"

"Look," he said, standing, "I'm not here to give you any second thoughts. I, uh, might want to come back and talk to your husband. Would you tell him that?"

"Of course," she said. "Where are you staying?"

"The Diamond Palace."

"Of course."

Clint headed for the door.

"Mr. Adams."

"Yes."

"Lillian Kingsforth."

"What about her."

"She's a little . . . skittish when it comes to business," she said. "Her husband always handled everything. Once she took over, the hotel started going downhill. When we offered to buy, we were doing her a favor."

"And you?"

"What do you mean?"

"If your husband died," Clint said, "you'd be in the same position, right? He handles all the business? Would you sell?"

She opened her mouth, but an answer didn't come out.

"Would you be a little . . . skittish about business?" he asked. "Or are you skittish already? And that's why your husband handles everything."

"I—my husband tells me everything."

"Of course he does," Clint said and left.

TWENTY-TWO

Clint went to see the Brit next, Adrian Webster. He had
an office in a building in a section of Market Street that
catered to businessmen. On the door it said WEBSTER
HOLDINGS. The secretary seated behind a desk was in her
fifties, very spinsterish in appearance—black hair streaked
with gray and worn atop her head—and very British.

"May I help you, sir?" she asked.

"I'd like to see Mr. Webster, please."

She looked Clint up and down, disapprovingly.

"Do you have an appointment?" she asked.

"You know I don't," he said, "because you make all
his appointments."

"I have that privilege, sir," she said, "and Mr. Webster
never sees anyone without an appointment."

"But I think he'll see me."

"And why is that, sir?"

"Because my name is Clint Adams."

No sign of recognition.

"And . . . ?"

"And I'm here representing Mrs. Lillian Kingsforth."

That name she did recognize.

"Just a moment, please."

"Sure," he said. "Take your time."

The woman got up, went through the door behind her. After several minutes the door opened and she waved at him.

"Please, come in."

"Thank you."

He entered, saw the man seated behind the desk, and smelled the pipe tobacco in the air. There was a large window behind Adrian Webster.

"Mr. Webster, this is Clint Adams."

"Thank you, Sara Jane," Webster said. "That's all."

Clint could see the shine in the woman's eyes as she said, "Yes, sir." She was in love with her boss.

She left and closed the door.

"Have a seat, sir," Webster said. "Sara Jane tells me you're here representing Lillian Kingsforth. Extraordinary woman, that. Lovely."

Webster was in his mid-forties, with a full head of wavy black hair shiny with pomade. He had broad shoulders but small hands. Clint thought the man didn't stand because he was probably shorter than he'd like to be. The pomade in his hair made it stand up, adding to his height.

Clint walked to a chair in front of the man's desk and sat. The man didn't offer to shake hands. He was also self-conscious about their small size.

"Yes, she is lovely," Clint said, "and she was almost flattened."

"I beg your pardon?"

"Somebody tried to kill her," Clint said. "She's asked me to try to find out who."

"That's awful," Webster said. "How can I help you?"

"Well, you're one of the people who's been trying to buy her property."

Webster stared at Clint for a moment, then grinned and said, "And you think I would kill her because she turned me down? You're mad."

"Maybe."

"How was this attempt made?"

"She was walking down the street and a crate fell from a building, just missing her."

Webster spread his hands. "And do I look like the kind of man who would climb up on top of a building and push a crate off?"

Clint didn't know if Webster was saying that he wasn't physically able or that he was too well dressed to do it.

"You could have had it done for you," Clint said.

"Are you serious?"

"I'm just asking questions, Mr. Webster," Clint said. "How badly do you want the Diamond Palace?"

"Not badly enough to kill for it, I can tell you that, sir."

"What about Peter Forrest?"

"What about him?"

"Do you think he'd kill for a piece of property?"

"Of course not."

"Or the Garvins?"

"This is preposterous," Webster said. "Do the police know you are annoying prominent citizens this way?"

"I don't know," Clint said. "You'll have to ask them."

"Perhaps I will," Webster said, "because I don't believe I want to continue this conversation, at all."

"That's fine," Clint said, standing. "Thanks for seeing me."

Clint left and found Sara Jane seated at her desk.

"Sara Jane what?" he asked.

"I beg your pardon?"

"What's your last name?"

She stared at him a moment, her eyes magnified slightly by her eyeglasses. Her eyes were brown, and probably her prettiest feature, even in her fifties.

"Halligan," she said.

"Well, Miss—is it 'Miss'?"

"It is."

"Miss Halligan, I wonder if you'd have dinner with me tonight."

"I—what?"

"Dinner? You do eat dinner, don't you?"

"Well, yes, but . . ."

He didn't know if she was taken aback by his invitation because of her age and appearance, or because she was insulted that he'd ask when they had just met.

"I'm staying at the Diamond Palace hotel," he said. "If you'd like to accept my invitation, we could meet in the lobby at seven. Afterward, I promise to see you safely home."

"Well, I don't—I can't—"

"I hope to see you then," he said and left the office.

Outside he stopped for a moment on the street to see if she'd follow. She didn't. What she'd probably do is tell her boss about the invitation. If she did show up, it might be because Webster told her to.

It would be interesting to see what happened.

TWENTY-THREE

Clint left Peter Forrest for last, since his office was in Portsmouth Square, and that would put him closest to the Diamond Palace when he was done.

Forrest's place was unimaginatively called the Lucky Lady. It had it all—hotel, saloon, gaming. Clint wondered why they insisted on calling it "gaming" when everybody knew it was "gambling."

Rather than go to the hotel desk and ask for Forrest, he went to the bar in the saloon. Invariably the owners of these hotel gaming palaces left the running of the hotel to others. They were primarily interested in the gambling.

He ordered a beer at the already crowded bar. Unlike other parts of the city, business started early in Portsmouth Square—the business of drinking as well as gambling.

When the bartender brought the beer, Clint had to lean over the bar to be heard.

"I'm looking for Peter Forrest."

The bartender nodded and said, "He owns this place."

Patiently, Clint said, "I know, that's why I'm looking for him here. Where is he?"

"He's around, somewhere," the barman said. "He likes to make the rounds, watch the games, talk to the people. If you stay right there he'll eventually come to the bar."

"Okay," Clint said, "let me know when he shows up."

Clint wanted to get back to his hotel to see if Sara Jane was actually going to meet him there. She probably knew all of her boss's business, and maybe he could find out something from her. Meanwhile, Webster might tell to her to keep their date and try to find out something from him.

Clint nursed the beer and watched the games he could see from the bar, as well as the girls working the floor. Forrest seemed to like to hire them young. He didn't think there was a girl there older than twenty-one or twenty-two.

Clint was about to turn around and ask for another beer when he felt a tap on his shoulder.

"Here comes the boss now," the bartender said, leaning over so he could say it in Clint's ear. Clint looked at him and the man pointed with his chin. Clint looked, saw a man in his thirties, tall and slender, walking toward him—or toward the bar.

"Introduce me," Clint said.

"Barry," Forrest called, "a beer."

"Sure, Boss," the bartender said. "This fella wants to see you."

"What about?" Peter Forrest asked, looking at Clint. "You got a complaint about a game? I've got a manager for that."

"Not about a game," Clint said. "This is about Lily Kingsforth."

Forrest reached for his beer without taking his eyes off Clint.

"What about her? Does she want to sell? She send you with an offer?"

"Not exactly."

"That bitch is makin' a big mistake, fella," Forrest said. "You tell her that."

"I don't think I like your mouth."

"Yeah, well, fuck you, too," Forrest said. "How's that?"

"Not nice."

As Forrest started to lift the beer mug to his mouth, Clint drove the heel of his left hand into the bottom of the glass. The force drove the glass into Forrest's face like a missile. If the mug hadn't been so thick the glass might have broken. As it was, he heard some teeth break and stepped back to avoid blood spray.

"Hey, Jesus!" the bartender said. "What the hell—"

Clint clapped both hands over Peter Forrest's ears and the man fell to the floor, holding his face. Ribbons of red flowed from between his fingers.

"You better get your boss a doctor," Clint said.

"You're in trouble, mister," the bartender said.

"Well, your boss will want to know my name," Clint said, as onlookers started to lean over to take a look at the injured man. "You tell him Clint Adams is staying at the Diamond Palace, if he wants to come over and do something about this. Got it?"

"Clint Adams?" the bartender said. "I, uh, I didn't know—"

"You didn't bother to ask," Clint said, "and neither did he. Tell him I'll be back to finish our conversation, and he better be ready to answer some questions."

"Jeez, sure, Mr. Adams, sure."

Clint took one last look at the foul-mouthed Peter Forrest. The man was still on the floor, trying to hold his jaw in place. If it was broken, he was going to have a hard time answering questions.

TWENTY-FOUR

Clint went back to his hotel room, washed, and changed his clothes just in case Sara Jane did show up. He was going to pump her for information, but that didn't mean he wasn't going to act like a gentleman.

When he got down to the lobby, he was surprised to find her already there. She had changed from her business attire into a dress and had let her hair down. She still appeared to be middle-aged, but she looked younger than she had at the office.

"Sorry I'm late," he said.

"You're not," she said. "I was early. I'm a bit . . . nervous."

"Why's that?"

"It's been a long time since a man invited me out."

"I can't believe that."

"You're sweet," she said. "Where will we be going to eat?"

"Well," he said, "I didn't expect you to get so dressed up, so for someone as lovely as you, it'll have to be someplace special."

"Oh," she said, "I'm going to have to be careful with you."

Of all the gambling houses in Portsmouth Square the Varsouvienne had one of the best kitchens and dining rooms. Clint took Sara Jane there, and she was suitably impressed.

"Doesn't your boss take you out to eat?" he asked.

"Only for lunch, and only business luncheons," she said.

"You mean you and he aren't . . ."

"Oh, no," she said.

"Is he married?"

"No, but he likes his women younger and more glamorous," she said.

"Then he's a fool."

"There you go again," she said. "Shouldn't we order?"

"Sure," he said. "Order anything you want."

"Aren't we going to try to get some information out of each other?" she asked. "I mean, isn't that why you actually invited me?"

"And isn't that why you came?" he asked. "Yes, we're going to do that, but let's eat first."

Over dinner he found out how long she had been in San Francisco and how long she had been working for Adrian Webster.

"He came to this country ten years ago," she said. "At that time I was ready to stop working in banking, so I applied for the job with him and got it."

"And have you been happy in your job?"

"Yes, very," she said. "He pays me well."

"And are you in love with him?"

"Well, you really get to the point, don't you?" she asked. "No, I'm not in love with him. That wouldn't be right."

"Because he's younger?"

She smiled.

"Oh, no," she said, "I like younger men very much. No, it's because he's my boss."

"And if he wasn't your boss?"

"But he is," she said.

And that seemed to be the end of the subject.

Over dessert she tried to find out how he felt about being the Gunsmith. He dodged the question as long as he could.

"You really don't like talking about this, do you?" she asked.

"No," he said, "but that doesn't matter. It is what it is."

"And you have to live with it."

"Right."

"What if you hadn't become the Gunsmith?"

"But I did," he said, "and I am."

And that was the end of that.

After dessert she said, "Well, that was a wonderful meal. Thank you."

"You're welcome."

They left the dining room, walked through the lobby, and out the front door.

"Cab, sir?" a doorman asked.

"I'll see you home," he said to Sara Jane.

"But I'm not ready to go home."

"Do you want to do some gambling?"

"I don't gamble."

"Then what—"

"I want to go back to your hotel."

He stared at her, and she smiled.

"I told you I like younger men."

TWENTY-FIVE

When Clint entered the lobby of the Diamond Palace with Sara Jane, he saw Lily standing at the front desk with the clerk who had checked him in. It seemed like the poor kid was the only clerk in the place.

She frowned when she looked over at him, and he simply nodded and then went up the stairs after Sara Jane.

When they got to his room, he unlocked the door and allowed her to precede him. Inside he turned up the gas lamp on the wall, then removed the Colt New Line from behind his back. She watched him put the gun down on the dresser top.

"I hope that wasn't a problem for you," she said.

"What do you mean?"

"That was Mrs. Kingsforth down in the lobby, wasn't it?"

"Yes."

"And she saw us come up here."

"I don't think she'll evict me for that."

"That's not what I meant," Sara Jane said. "I thought perhaps you and she . . ."

"What? Oh, no," Clint said. "She owns the hotel, and I'm doing some work to try and help her, but we haven't ever . . . no."

"Good," she said, "I don't like poaching on other women's property."

"I'm no one's property," he said.

"You know," she said, undoing some buttons on the front of her dress, "I know what you thought when you first saw me."

"You do? What was I thinking?"

"Not bad-looking for a spinster," she said.

"I didn't—"

"Sure you did," she said. "That's what all men think when they walk into that office. But that's okay, it's what I want them to think."

She finished unbuttoning her dress and slid it down her waist, over her hips, and let it drop to the floor.

"But I'm not a spinster," she said. "I'm a widow. I was married once, a long time ago." She removed her undergarments, until she was standing there totally nude. He was surprised by her body. Big, rounded breasts and hips that she managed to hide beneath her clothes.

"He died, also a long time ago. Since then I pick and choose the men I want to be with. But I'll never again allow a man to get that close to me. It hurts too much when he leaves."

"Your husband died."

"I know he did," she said, with barely contained anger, "but he left me, nevertheless. But you're not going to leave me, Clint Adams."

She walked up to him and kept going until she bumped

into him. Her breasts were very firm for a woman her age.

"Not tonight, anyway."

Feeling the heat coming from her body he said, "Furthest thing from my mind."

TWENTY-SIX

Sara Jane's skin was remarkably smooth and fragrant. Clint kissed her shoulders, her neck, and then her mouth. He slid his hands up and down her back, then down to cup and knead her firm buttocks.

"Surprised?" she asked.

"I—what? How do you mean?"

"How old do you think I am?" she asked. "I'll bet you expected sagging breasts and buttocks."

"Sara Jane—"

"I know, I know, I look older dressed," she went on, kissing his neck and unbuttoning his shirt. "I dress so I'll look over fifty, but I'm not."

"Oh, well—"

"I'm only forty-nine," she said, sliding his shirt off. "Not as old as you thought, maybe, but still older than you."

She kissed his nipples, ran her tongue around them, then went to work on his belt.

"And," she said, pulling the belt free from the loops, "I'll bet you thought I hadn't had sex in a long time, and

I'd be grateful for the attention." She tossed the belt aside, undid the buttons on his trousers.

"Well, I didn't—"

"Oh, sure you did," she said, yanking his pants down almost angrily. "But I'm here to show you how wrong you were."

Clint wasn't sure he'd ever had sex before with a woman who angrily intending to prove a point. But he forgot all about it when Sara Jane got down on his knees and licked his rigid penis.

She took hold of his erection with both hands, stroked it, licked it from tip to shaft and back again, wetting it before finally taking it into her mouth and sucking it. She seemed very practiced and talented, so it was easy to believe that she had not gone without sex for any extended period of time.

She slid her hands up and down his legs, the backs of his thighs, then grabbed his buttocks and clenched her hands as she took the entire length of him into her mouth. Clint actually stood up on his toes and grabbed for her head when she did this.

Abruptly, she released his penis and sat back on her haunches.

"You look silly with your pants around your ankles and your boots still on," she said. "Why don't you take them off and join me on the bed?"

"You don't have to ask me twice."

She got on the bed and watched as he removed his boots and kicked them and the pants away.

"Have you known many young women who could take you into their mouths like that? The whole length?"

He didn't want to disappoint her by telling her that yes, he had run into some women who could do it.

As if she could read his mind she said, "And I don't mean whores."

"Well," he admitted, "I haven't met many secretaries who could do it."

She reached for him as he got into bed with her, but he pushed her away and down onto her back.

"My turn," he said. "You're not the only one who wants to show off."

"Be my guest," she said, projecting an attitude that indicated she didn't expect much. Clint had the feeling Sara Jane had been disappointed by men in a lot more ways than her husband dying on her. And he was the one who was going to have to prove himself different.

Peter Forrest returned to his Lucky Lady later that evening with his face stitched and bandaged. He didn't go into the saloon but instead went upstairs to his rooms. He was not anxious to see anyone or to be seen. Plus he was starving because he was not able to eat.

But although he couldn't eat, he was being eaten up on the inside by his anger. How dare Clint Adams blindside him like that? He was going to make sure the man paid for what he'd done, and if he was going to make him pay he might as well make Lily Kingsforth pay, as well. After all, she was the one who had sicced Adams onto him.

Forrest used his key to unlock his door and enter. He stopped short when he saw the person sitting in his armchair, waiting for him.

"What are you doing here?" he asked, but it came out muffled and he had to repeat himself, enunciating very carefully.

"I heard what happened," the person said, "and I

thought I should do something about it before you did something stupid."

"What . . . can . . . you . . . do?" Forrest asked, painfully forming the words.

"This."

"What the hell—" Forrest said, but it came out, "Whuh de hul—"

The person in the armchair pointed a gun at Forrest and fired once. The bullet went in just above the bandages, and lodged inside his head. Forrest fell to the floor, face-first. The shooter checked to make sure he was dead, then got out of there.

There was probably too much noise downstairs for anyone to have heard the shot or the fall, but the shooter didn't want to take any chances.

The shooter took the back staircase down and waited to make sure he wouldn't run into anyone in the hallway. The noise from the saloon and gaming hall was loud, reinforcing the belief that no one had heard what went on upstairs.

Forrest had become a liability, even before Adams had humiliated him. Left alive, he would definitely have done something stupid.

The shooter quickly moved to the back door and went outside.

TWENTY-SEVEN

Clint had Sara Jane on her hands and knees and was fucking her from behind. Her back was so smooth and beautiful that from this angle—if not for the gray in her hair—she could have been twenty years old.

She grunted as she drove her ass back into him, ground herself into him, rotated her hips before drawing away and then driving back again. At one point he was completely still and she was doing all the work, backing into him, sweating, growling, grunting with the effort. She not only looked younger from this angle, but she had the sexual appetite of a much younger woman. It was a shame she was so angry at men.

Clint loved women. He loved being around them and he loved making love to them. He didn't think he could do it too well if he hated them. This made him wonder how good sex with Sara Jane would be if she loved men.

She disengaged from him just long enough to flip herself over onto her back, then grabbed him and pulled him back to her. He drove himself into her, and she wrapped her legs around him.

"Fuck me hard!" she said urgently into his ear. "I may be an old lady, but I won't break."

"Stop fishing for compliments," he told her.

He slid his hands beneath her, held her, and starting slamming into her over and over again until it was he who was swearing and grunting.

She spoke to him while they rutted—that's what they were doing, not making love, not even fucking—but only in single words, like "damn," and "ooh," and "God," and "baby."

The more time he spent with her, the harder it was to think of her as the woman he'd seen in Adrian Webster's office.

She bit his shoulder, bringing him back from his reverie. This wasn't the woman from the office; this was Sara Jane, the woman with her teeth in his shoulder and her legs wrapped around his waist.

"God, you're so wet," he said to her. The sheet between them was soaked with her juices. "I want to taste you."

"Be my guest," she said. She removed her legs from around his waist and spread them as wide as she could, holding on to her ankles. She had a look of pride on her face. Let's see a woman twenty years younger do this!

Clint was tired of thinking. He got down between her legs and attacked her with his tongue and lips. Before long she was writhing and groaning and his face was shiny and wet with her.

"Oooh, God," she moaned, "you're sooooo good at that, aren't you?"

He didn't bother trying to answer. He was busy. He slid his hands beneath her ass and lifted her. Her juices had covered her ass cheeks and wet her anus. He licked up as much of it as he could, concentrating on her puckered pink orifice.

"Oh, Jesus," she said, writhing even more. He held her tightly, though, and continued to lick that hole, then moved again to her wet pussy. Before long she was jerking uncontrollably, gasping for air, trying to push him away and hold him there at the same time . . .

She still had not gotten her breath back when he climbed atop her and entered her again. She was so sensitive that she started to spasm again immediately. Wave after wave of orgasm rolled over her, and later she'd think back and realize that she had blacked out for a moment.

This was definitely not a typical man.

"I thought you were going to kill me," she said, later. She was sitting up, her arms wrapped around her knees.

"I just wanted to make sure you remembered me when I'm gone."

"Oh, I'll remember you, all right," she said. "You're the only man who ever licked my . . . I mean, I *never* felt anything like that before."

"Good, I'm glad."

"God." She lay back down on her back and slapped her hands down on the mattress. "Can you do that every time?" she asked.

"I think the question is," he said, "can *you* do that every time?"

She rolled over and smiled at him, reached down between his legs to take hold of him.

"I think we should check and see."

"I'm ready again," he said.

His penis was swelling in her hand and she said, "Oh, my, it is!"

TWENTY-EIGHT

There was a knock on the door the next morning to wake them both up.

"Who's that?" she asked, anxiously, rubbing her eyes. "Oh my God, we fell asleep?"

"I think we knocked each other out," he said.

"I can't be seen—" She pulled the sheet up to her chest.

"Don't worry," he said. "This is a big room and the bed can't be seen from the door." He patted her bare shoulder. "I'm not going to let anyone in."

When he stood up she thought he was reaching for his trousers, but instead he plucked his gun from his holster, which was hanging just above her.

"Wha—"

"Can't be too careful," he said.

"But . . . you're still naked."

He smiled and said, "That's what they get for waking me up."

When he opened the door he startled both Inspectors Burns and Logan.

"Whoa!" Logan said.

Clint didn't know what startled them more, his nudity or the gun in his hand.

"Don't shoot," Burns said.

"What the hell—" Clint said. "It's early."

"Not too early for murder," Burns said.

"Who got murdered?"

"Why don't you get dressed and come downstairs and we'll talk about it," Logan said.

"And leave the gun," Burns said. "And tell whoever's in there with you we apologize for waking her."

They started down the hall to the stairs and he closed the door.

"Who was that?" she asked.

"The police."

"What did they want?"

"They want to talk to me about somebody who got killed last night."

"Who?" she asked, curiously.

"I'll have to get dressed and go downstairs to find out," he said. "Why don't you wait here?"

"I have to go," she said.

"If you walk through the hall, they'll see you," he said. "Why not wait until I get rid of them? I'll come back up and tell you what's going on."

"Who could've been murdered?" she asked.

"I don't know," he said, getting dressed. "I talked to a lot of people yesterday."

"Do you think it's Mr. Webster?" She was suddenly alarmed.

"I don't know, Sara Jane," he said. "If it is, I'll come right up and tell you. If I'm not right back, you'll know it's not your boss. Why don't you take a nice hot bath, and I'll be back as soon as I can."

"All right," she said. "A bath sounds nice."

Fully dressed, he walked to the bed and kissed her. The morning light showed the lines at the corner of her eyes and mouth, but she still looked lovely. He kissed her, then went to the dresser for the New Line.

"Stay out of sight," he told her, tucking the gun behind his back. He grabbed a jacket and put it on to cover the gun. "I'll be back as soon as I can."

"Okay."

She was still sitting in the bed when he left, but had let the sheet drop from her. Her dark brown nipples stayed with him all the way down to the lobby.

TWENTY-NINE

He found the two inspectors waiting for him in the lobby.

"No six-gun?" Logan asked.

Clint didn't answer.

"Why don't we get some coffee?" Burns suggested.

"First tell me who's dead," Clint insisted.

The two policemen exchanged a glance, and then Burns said, "Peter Forrest, if it makes a difference."

"Okay," Clint said, "let's get some coffee."

Once they were in the dining room with coffee in front of them Clint said, "What's going on?"

"We just have a few questions," Burns said.

Clint turned his head and saw Lily sitting at her table. She smiled and he nodded.

"About what?"

"When Peter Forrest was found he'd been shot," Burns said, "but his face was bandaged. He'd been attacked before he was killed—hours before."

"We heard you had something to do with that," Logan said.

"I did," Clint said, "and I can tell you about it, but I had nothing to do with him getting killed."

"Okay," Burns said, "let's start with how his face got like that."

Clint told them about his visit to Peter Forrest's saloon, his conversation, and how it ended.

"You know," Burns said, "if he was alive and wanted to press charges, I'd have to take you in."

"I know that."

"So you lucked out that he's dead," Logan said.

Clint looked at the younger man.

"You really think I'd kill him to keep him from filing a complaint against me?"

"Men have killed for lesser reasons," Burns said, "but never mind. Who else did you talk to yesterday?"

Clint told him. "Any of them turn up dead?" he asked Burns.

"Not yet," Burns said.

"So you think he's dead because I talked to him?" Clint asked.

"Who knows?" Logan said. "The other saloon owner got killed after you talked to him."

"I never talked to him," Clint said.

"Oh, yeah, you said that," Logan answered.

"No progress on that murder?"

"No," Burns said, "and now we've got this one to work on."

"Where's your boss?"

"Oh, he'll be around," Burns said. "He likes working on murders."

Clint finished his coffee. "So where do we stand?" he asked. "Are you taking me in?"

"Not today," Burns said. "Nobody saw you around the Lucky Lady after you left."

"That where Forrest was killed?"

Burns nodded.

"It happened upstairs in his rooms."

"Somebody break in?"

"Doesn't look like it," Burns said. "but it looks like somebody might have been waitin' for him when he got back from the doctor."

"You broke his jaw," Logan said, "and knocked out a bunch of teeth."

"He should've watched his mouth, then," Clint said.

"What'd he say?" Logan asked.

"Something unflattering about a friend of mine."

"A lady?" Burns asked.

"Yes."

Burns shrugged, as if that answered that.

"Okay," the older inspector said. "We're done . . . for now."

All three men stood up.

"You boys know the way out," Clint said. "I have to talk to someone else."

"Okay. We'll be around, Adams," Burns said. "And my boss will probably come by to talk to you."

"That's fine," Clint said. "I'll tell him the same thing I told you, the truth."

"He'll love that," Logan said.

Clint watched the two inspectors leave, then turned and walked to Lily's table.

"Mind if I sit?"

"Don't you have . . . company upstairs?" she asked.

"I'm more concerned with the company I just had down here," he said. "They were the police."

"And why were they here?"

"Because somebody killed Peter Forrest last night."

She looked shocked.

"Okay," she said, "maybe you should sit down."

THIRTY

Lily poured Clint a cup of coffee.

"What happened?"

"I had gone to talk to him earlier in the evening," Clint said. "We had . . . an altercation."

"What kind of altercation?"

"I broke his jaw."

She looked surprised.

"What was that about?"

"Let's just say he said something that offended me."

"I wouldn't have taken you for the kind of man who can be offended."

"Well, he said something about you."

That surprised her, too. "Oh!"

"Don't ask me what he said," Clint added. "It was bad enough for me to break his jaw."

"But you didn't kill him?"

"I didn't hire out to kill your competition, Lily," he said.

"That's not what I wanted you to do, Clint," she said. "Do you think he had anything to do with trying to kill me?"

"I couldn't tell from the short time we talked," Clint said. "I was going to go back and talk to him again, but that's out, now."

"What about the others?"

"I talked to everyone," he said, "that is, everyone but Harold Garvin. I did talk to his wife, Chris."

"Oh, my," she said, "I forgot to tell you about her, didn't I?"

"Yes," he said. "I thought they were partners, but I found out they're man and wife."

"I'm sorry."

"It doesn't matter," he said. "She doesn't seem to know much about their business."

"No, apparently he takes care of all of that."

"Wouldn't you think he'd be lying to her, then?" he asked.

"Why would he do that?"

"Did your husband tell you everything?"

"Well, I'm sure he told me what I needed to know."

"That's probably what Harold Garvin does," Clint said.

"And you think that's lying?"

"Maybe by omission," he said.

"Well, I wasn't really my husband's business partner," she said. "Whereas, I believe Chris is."

"Well, she's a partner who never goes to business meetings, so I think it would be pretty easy for him to keep something from her."

"You mean like trying to kill me?"

"Yeah, something like that."

"Are you going to have trouble with the police?" she asked.

"No," he said, "I'm actually getting along pretty good

with the police. There should be a Lieutenant Hargrove here later looking for me."

"Do I tell him where you are?"

"If you know, yes."

"And what about the woman you came in here with last night?"

"You didn't recognize her?"

"No, I didn't."

"Do you know Adrian Webster's secretary?"

"Sara Jane? Yes, we've—wait a minute. That was Sara Jane?"

"It was."

"But she looked so . . . different."

"Out of the office, I guess she does," he said.

"So you were with her . . ."

"To try and get some information about her boss."

"And did you?"

"Not really," he said, standing up, "but I'm not done trying, yet. I'll see you later, Lily."

When he got back to the room, Sara Jane had taken her bath and gotten dressed.

"Who got killed?" she asked, anxiously.

"Peter Forrest. Do you know him?"

"I know of him, of course," she said, "but I've never met him."

"Well, somebody killed him at home, after I saw him," Clint said. "The police just wanted to ask me a few questions."

"Is everything all right?"

"Yes."

"I need to go," she said. "The bath was fine, but I need to change clothes and go to work."

"Can I see you again?" he asked.

"If you'd like to," she said. "We, uh, weren't very good at pumping each other for information, were we?"

"No," he said, "but we were pretty good, anyway."

THIRTY-ONE

Clint was trying to figure his next move when there was a knock at his door. He expected it to be Lieutenant Hargrove, but when he opened it he found a bellboy standing there.

"Telegram for you, sir."

"Thank you," Clint said, giving the boy two bits.

"Thanks!"

The telegram was from William Pinkerton, asking Clint if he would please remain in San Francisco for a few more days, in the hopes that he would still be contacted.

Clint folded the telegram and stuffed it into his saddlebag. There was no decision for him to make, since the police had already *told* him to stay in town until the first murder was solved, and now there had been a second. If not for that, he would have sent a missive back to Pinkerton telling him sorry, but he'd already wasted too much time on this wild-goose chase.

And then there was the dead man in the street. Was that a complete coincidence? Was he connected to the other two murders? If, indeed, those two murders were even connected. Or did he have something to do with the whole Pinkerton thing?

Then he had a thought. Allan Pinkerton, while a patriot and a great detective, was also a duplicitous son of a bitch when he needed to get something done. What if this had all been a ruse on William Pinkerton's part just to get Clint out to San Francisco? And if so, why? With William and Robert, Clint had no idea how far from the tree the apples had fallen. He didn't know the two men well enough to gauge. But if they were anything like their father, then he wouldn't put it past them to trick him into coming out here.

Before he could give the matter any more thought, there was another knock on the door. This time it was the lieutenant.

"Do you have time for a talk, Mr. Adams?" the man asked, politely.

Clint, sensing the change in attitude, said, "Since you ask so nicely, sure."

"Coffee in the dining room?"

"Why not?" Clint asked. "It seems a popular choice."

They walked down to the lobby in silence and were seated in the dining room. They ordered coffee and sat back, regarding each other. Clint decided to make it easy on the man.

"So, you've either been told to lay off me, or you've decided I'm not guilty of anything."

"A little bit of both, actually," Hargrove said. "I never seriously considered you a suspect. I know your reputation, and nothing indicates to me that you'd come to San Francisco to kill a third-rate saloon owner."

"What about the owner of a first-rate saloon, like Peter Forrest?"

"While the Lucky Lady may have been considered first rate," Hargrove said, "to my mind Peter Forrest was just another third-rate owner. And no, I don't think you killed him, either."

"Why not?"

"Again, your reputation doesn't show any willingness to ambush men in their homes. I suspect if you wanted to kill him, you could have done it earlier, when you broke a beer mug in his face."

"I didn't intend the mug to break," Clint said. "Maybe the Lucky Lady isn't so first rate."

"It wouldn't surprise me."

The waiter came over with a pot of coffee and two cups—excellent china, Clint noticed. The man poured for them and then withdrew.

"You said a little bit of both."

"My boss has not only told me to lay off you as a suspect, but to try to solicit your help in solving these murders."

"I'm not a detective."

"That's not what we heard."

"Well, that's what I'm telling you."

The lieutenant frowned.

"So you won't help?"

"Am I still instructed to stay in San Francisco?" Clint asked.

"No, you're free to leave whenever you like."

Now that he was committed to helping Lily Kingsforth there was no way Clint could just leave.

"So what do you say?"

"I'm committed to something else," Clint said, "but I don't see why I couldn't lend a hand."

"You'll work with my inspectors?"

"Burns and Logan?"

The man nodded.

"Logan's a little full of himself, but I like Burns," Clint said. "Let's say I'll coordinate with them."

"I'm instructed to tell you to play it however you want to," Hargrove said.

"This doesn't make you happy, does it?"

"No," Hargrove said, candidly, "it doesn't, but my goal is to catch a killer, and I don't much care how it gets done."

If Clint managed to catch the killer, or figure out who it was, that could only reflect well on Hargrove and his men. If Clint failed, that wouldn't bother Hargrove much, either. The lieutenant was in a win-win situation, and Clint was experienced enough with life to know that you always took advantage of such situations.

"Please understand," Hargrove said, "I have nothing against you. In fact, I have a great deal of respect for you, but this is my backyard."

"Understood," Clint said. "I am perfectly willing to do what you want me to do—help, or stay out of it."

"What I want has nothing to do with anything," Hargrove said, "except that, as I said, I want to catch a killer."

"Or killers."

"Yes," Hargrove said, "there is always that possibility, isn't there?"

THIRTY-TWO

This time Clint walked the policeman out to the lobby, where they split up. Hargrove went out the front door and Clint walked to the front desk.

"Can you send a telegram for me?" he asked the clerk.

"I'll have it done, sir."

Clint wrote out a message to William Pinkerton, basically telling the man he'd stay in San Francisco a few more days. He didn't bother to tell him why.

"Thank you," he said, handing the message to the clerk.

"Certainly, Mr. Adams."

Clint was turning to leave when the clerk said, "Uh, sir?"

"Yes?"

The clerk looked both ways and behind Clint, then risked a look behind himself before leaning over the desk and lowering his voice.

"There was a man in the lobby earlier," he said, "who watched you and the lieutenant go into the dining room."

"What did he look like?"

"In his thirties, dark hair, rather disheveled, not well dressed at all."

"And where did he go?"

"After you and the lieutenant went into the dining room he waited for about fifteen minutes, then left."

"Well, if you see him again, try to get his name."

"How do I do that, sir?"

"Ask him."

"Um, ask him?"

"You should probably find out who he is and if you can help him, right?" Clint asked. "I mean, you'd do that with anyone, wouldn't you?"

"Well . . . I suppose so."

"And if I'm around," Clint said, "send somebody to find me."

"Yes, sir."

"If you don't want to ask who he is, tell your boss," Clint said. "I'm sure she'll do it."

"Oh, yes, sir. Mrs. Kingsforth is not afraid of anyone."

"I can believe that," Clint said. "Thanks for the information."

"Oh, yes, sir," the man said, puffing out his chest. "You can count on me."

"I know I can."

He turned and headed for the door.

Outside Lieutenant Hargrove found Burns and Logan waiting across the street. He crossed over and joined them in front of another hotel.

"So what do you think?" Burns asked.

"He didn't do it," Hargrove said.

"But does he know anything?" Logan asked.

"If he does, he's agreed to help us," the lieutenant said.

"You must have mixed feelings about that, Lieutenant," Burns said.

"You got that right," Hargrove said. "I don't want some amateur meddling in our case, but then again, he is the Gunsmith."

"He's not a detective," Logan said.

"And he freely admits that, himself," Hargrove said. "But he might be of some help, so you boys are gonna work with him."

"You mean he's gonna work with us, don't ya?" Logan asked.

"However you need to look at it," Hargrove said. "Just catch me a killer."

Hargrove walked away. Burns turned to Logan and said, "Or killers."

Clint stopped just outside the front door to get his bearings.

Eddie MacDonald, dead.

Walter Trench, dead.

Peter Forrest, dead.

And somebody tried to kill Lily Kingsforth.

But what about her husband? He had died two years ago, but how? Could a death two years earlier be connected to these?

And were these connected to the Diamond Palace, or to Allan Pinkerton, who had died at least four years earlier?

He needed as much information on the dead men as possible, and he decided to start with Lily's husband. Clint needed to know when he died and how.

More than that he needed to know what his name was and who he was.

THIRTY-THREE

Clint found Lily in her office.

"Developments already?" she asked, as he walked in.

"If you call being asked by the police to help developments, then I guess the answer is yes," he said, seating himself across from her.

"What? Well, does that mean you're not a suspect?" she asked.

"Looks like it does."

She sat back in her chair. "But you're still working for me, right?"

"Definitely," he said, "but I'm wondering if all of these murders are connected."

"How do you propose to find out?"

"By asking questions."

"Starting with me?"

"Well," he said, "I never did find out your husband's name or how he died."

A pained look passed over her face.

"I'm sorry to bring up painful memories," he said.

"No, that's all right," she said. "His name was Paul and he was killed one night, down the street from here."

"Killed how?"

"He was robbed," she said. "And stabbed."

"And what did the police find out?"

"Nothing," she said. "They never found who did it."

"That's interesting," he said.

"You think there's a connection?"

Clint hesitated.

"Clint, we *can* talk about this," she said.

"All right," Clint said, "how soon after Paul was killed did you start getting offers for the hotel?"

"The following week."

"Who from?"

"Peter Forrest," she said. "He said he was willing to take it off my hands to help me out."

"And then the others?"

"Yes."

"And you turned them down."

"Right," she said, "and they've come back from time to time over the past two years."

"With better offers each time?"

"Yes."

He stopped to think.

"You can't think that Paul's death two years ago . . ."

"What if that's when it all started?" he asked.

"And now," she asked, "after two years they've decided to kill each other off?"

"Well, Forrest is dead," he said. "The other two murders may not be connected."

"Other two?"

He told her about Eddie MacDonald on Market Street

and Walter Trench in the street not far from where they were now.

"How would those be connected?"

"I don't know," he said, "but coincidences just don't sit right with me."

"So one of these bastards—or that bitch—killed my husband?"

"It's possible."

A single tear made its way down her cheek. She wiped it away angrily with her palm.

"I thought I was over this."

"And how do you get over something like that?" he asked.

She wiped away another tear.

"I guess you don't."

THIRTY-FOUR

Clint left Lily with her tears still flowing. He felt bad about it, but he decided to give her some time alone.

Outside he looked across the street and saw Inspectors Burn and Logan standing in front of another hotel. He crossed over to them.

"You fellows waiting for me to follow me?" he asked.

"No," Burns said, "we were told that we're gonna be workin' together."

"We just thought we'd wait out here for you," Logan said.

"Good," Clint said, "because I have some questions."

"Why don't we go have a drink and you can ask them," Burns suggested.

Logan said, "There's a little place down the street that doesn't have any of that annoying gambling noise."

"I suspect you're not a gambler," Clint said.

"I got other things to do with my money," Logan said, "not that I've got any."

"Come on," Burns said, "Adams is buyin'."

* * *

It was a small saloon—no gambling, no hotel. A few tables, a small, intimate bar, empty this time of the day.

They got three beers and walked to a back table.

"What can you tell me about the murder of Paul Kingsforth?" Clint asked.

"Who?" Logan asked.

"Lillian Kingsforth's husband," Burns said. "He was murdered on the street two years ago." Burns looked at Clint. "Logan wasn't here, then."

"Okay," Clint said, "what can you tell me?"

"Not much," Burns said. "He was attacked on the street, pulled into an alley, stabbed to death, and robbed."

"By more than one person?"

"That's the way it looked."

"What'd they take?"

"His wallet."

"What about his watch? Or other jewelry?"

"He still had a watch and a ring."

"Why would someone rob him and leave the jewelry?" Clint asked.

Burns shrugged.

"Maybe they just wanted the cash," Logan said. "Maybe he was gambling, he won, and somebody followed him to take his cash."

"Or maybe somebody followed him," Clint said, "killed him, and grabbed the wallet to make it look like a robbery."

"And didn't think to take the jewelry?" Burns asked.

Clint nodded.

"Are you trying to connect Paul Kingsforth's murder with Peter Forrest's?" Burns asked.

"Kingsforth owned the Diamond Palace, and Forrest is one of the people who wanted it."

"Why kill them two years apart?" Burns asked.

"Somebody's been patient," Clint said. "Lily says she has continued to get offers over the past two years."

"So why suddenly become impatient?" Logan asked.

"And how does killing Forrest help anybody get the Diamond Palace if Lily Kingsforth is still not willing to sell it?" Burns asked.

"His wife told me that you were trying to blame her for the murder," Clint said.

"We looked into the possibility that she hired it done," Burns said. "After all, she ended up with all his money and the hotel."

"But?"

Burns shrugged. "In the end we couldn't connect her to it. All that means is if she hired it done, we couldn't find the man she hired."

"What about the other two murders?" Logan asked. "Any connection?"

"I have an idea," Clint said.

"What?" Burns said.

"Let's split up," he said. "I'll work on the Forrest killing. Burns, you can work on Eddie MacDonald, and young Logan here can work on Trench."

"How does splitting up benefit us?" Burns asked.

"Maybe," Clint said, "we can catch a killer before somebody else dies."

They discussed the logistics of Clint's idea for a three-part investigation.

"We just have to get together each evening and compare notes," Clint said.

"How many evenings?" Logan asked.

"Hopefully, it won't take that many," Clint said.

"And what about the Paul Kingsforth killing?" Burns asked.

"Well, it happened two years ago," Clint said. "Hopefully, if it is related, we'll be able to find out."

Burns and Logan exchanged a glance, and then the older inspector said, "What do we have to lose?"

"I'm going over to the Lucky Lady now," Clint said. "I want to find out who's running the place now that Forrest is dead."

"Okay," Burns said, "I'll go over to Eddie MacDonald's and nose around."

"Do you have a home address for Trench?" Clint asked Logan.

"Yeah, we do."

Clint made a spur-of-the-moment decision.

"Okay, well, I've got something to tell you that I only found out yesterday."

"What's that?" Logan asked.

"Trench was a Pinkerton."

"What?"

"He was working something on the Barbary Coast."

"How did you find that out?" Burns asked. "Or did you just recognize him because you're a Pinkerton, too?"

"No," Clint said. "I didn't lie about that. I'm not a Pinkerton and I didn't recognize him, but I do know the Pinkertons. I knew Allan, and I know his sons, Robert and William. Trench's partner knew that and came to me with the information."

"Why you and not us?" Burns asked.

"She's young and didn't know what to do."

"What did you tell her to do?" Logan asked.

"I told her to contact her boss, William Pinkerton in

Chicago, and get instructions. If I know him, he'll tell her to go to the police."

"Okay," Burns said, "I'll leave word that if she does come to us, we should be notified."

"So you think Trench's death may be connected to these others?" Logan asked.

"I wouldn't say that," Clint said. "Some of these people own property on the Barbary Coast—especially the Garvins.

"Okay," Logan said, "so I'll check them out."

"Harold and Chris," Clint said. "Chris is Christine. They're husband and wife."

Logan nodded. They finished their beers and walked outside.

"So when do we meet?" Logan asked. "And where?"

"How about here?" Clint asked. "Nine p.m. tonight?"

"Works for me," Burns said.

Logan nodded.

"I hope this works," Burns said. "The boss told us we should cooperate but . . ."

"If you have another idea," Clint said, "I'm open to it."

"Nope," Burns said, "no other ideas. I'm just hoping this one pans out."

"Believe me," Clint said, "so am I."

THIRTY-FIVE

Clint liked the changed situation. He only had to concentrate on one murder, Peter Forrest. If only one of them was connected to the attempt on Lily, Clint's money was on that one. Also, it might be the one connected to her husband's death.

He walked over to the Lucky Lady, which, like all the Portsmouth Square gaming halls, was in full swing despite the hour. All that would happen after dark is that it would get even more crowded.

Clint walked up to the bar and saw a different bartender than the last time he was there.

"Where's the bartender who was here last night?" he asked.

"Home, I guess," the man said. "He'll be here later."

"Who's taking over now that your boss is dead?" Clint asked.

"Why are you interested?"

"My name's Clint Adams," Clint said. "I'm working with the law on this."

The man became cooperative. Clint didn't know if it was his name or mention of the law.

"Barry, the other bartender, he'll be here at seven," the man said. "As far as who runs the place, the manager's name is Otis Corbin. I—I guess he'll be running it for a while."

"Where is he?"

"He's up in Mr. Forrest's office right now."

"Okay, thanks," Clint said. "I'm going up there."

"Sure."

Clint went up the stairs to Forrest's office, almost knocked, but decided to enter without doing so. There was a man behind the desk, going through the drawers. He was a short, rotund man in his fifties, with a bald head that gleamed in the light from the lamp on the desk. There were no windows in the room.

As Clint entered, the man straightened quickly and stared at Clint, wide-eyed.

"Who are you?" he asked. "Whaddaya want?"

"My name's Clint Adams," Clint said, "and I'm interested in who killed your boss."

"Are you with the law?"

"Yes."

"Where's your badge?"

"I don't have a badge," he said. "I'm working with them."

"Clint Adams, you said?"

"That's right."

The man's eyes went wide.

"You're the one who hurt Peter, messed up his face," Corbin said. "Y-you didn't come back and kill him?"

"No."

"H-how do I know that?"

"I'm not in jail," Clint said. "Instead I'm working with the police."

"H-how do I know *that*?"

"Because I'm telling you," Clint said. "That's going to have to be good enough, for now. What are you doing going through your bosses desk?"

"Huh? Somebody has to run things until . . ."

"Until what?"

Corbin shrugged.

"I don't know. Until we find out who's in charge."

"Did your boss have family?"

"Not that I know of."

"Partners?"

"That's what I'm tryin' to find out now," Corbin said. "If he had partners, there should be some papers here."

"I see."

"I—I have to keep lookin'."

"I know," Clint said, "but I'm going to help you."

"Why?"

"Because if he had partners," Clint answered, "I want to talk to them."

"If he had partners, you think that's who killed him?" Otis Corbin asked.

"Somebody with a motive had to have killed him," Clint said. "Did you have a motive?"

"M-me?" Corbin looked appalled. "N-no, why would I kill him?"

"I don't know," Clint said. "That's what I'm asking."

"N-no," Corbin said. "I didn't have a motive. He gave me a job when nobody else would."

"Okay, then if he has partners, they had a motive," Clint said.

"I-I suppose."

Clint walked to the desk, then looked over at a file cabinet in the corner.

"You keep going through the desk," Clint said, "and I'll go through the cabinet. What am I looking for?"

"Partnership papers," Corbin said, "signed by all the partners."

"Okay," Clint said, "let's get to work."

It took a few hours, but Clint finally came across the papers in the bottom drawer of the cabinet.

"Is this what we're looking for?" Clint asked, turning and holding them out.

Corbin turned, squinted, then stumbled as he reached for the papers. He grabbed them and held them close to his face.

"This is them," he said. "Partnership papers."

"Okay," Clint said. "Then who are the partners?"

Corbin held the papers to his chest.

"I don't know if I should—"

"We're past that now, Otis," Clint said. "Who are his partners?"

"All right, all right," Corbin said. "Let me look."

He took the papers to the light on the desk, leafed through them, and found what he wanted.

"How many?" Clint asked.

"Two," Otis said. "But they have the same last name."

"Harold and Christine Garvin?"

Corbin looked up at Clint in surprise and asked, "How did you know that?"

THIRTY-SIX

Clint told Otis Corbin to go ahead and keep running things.

"I'll let you know what happens," Clint said.

"But where are you going?"

"To see the partners."

Back to the Barbary Coast address of Harold and Christine Garvin. Clint entered the Coast Hotel and presented himself to the same clerk.

"Oh, hello."

"I'd like to see Mr. or Mrs. Garvin," Clint said.

"Oh, uh, well . . ."

"Are they both here?"

"Yes, sir, but—"

"Tell them."

"Sir, I—"

"Just tell them," Clint said. "I'll wait here."

"Yes, sir."

The clerk went back to the office and returned in

moments. He didn't look confident as he got back behind the desk.

"Um, Mr. Adams, sir," he said, "Mr. and Mrs. Garvin don't wish to speak with you."

"That a fact?"

"Yes, sir," the clerk said. "They said if you wish to talk to them you should come back with the police."

"We'll see about that."

Clint started back to the office and the clerk made no effort to stop him. When Clint reached the office, he kicked the door open and rushed inside. He looked around and found it empty, but that was okay. The Garvins may have run out a back door, but he spent the next half hour ransacking the office, looking for paperwork similar to what he'd found in Peter Forrest's office. For one thing they'd have to have a copy of their partnership agreement with Forrest. And for another they'd have partnership agreements with anyone they were in business with, and that's what he wanted to find out.

But after half an hour he found nothing, not even the agreement with Forrest. They must have had their paperwork stashed someplace else.

To make them pay for avoiding him he continued to destroy the office, including reducing their desk to splinters.

After that he went back outside. He had to give the young clerk credit. He had stuck around, even though he could probably hear the destruction going on in the office.

"Where do your bosses live?" he demanded.

"Uh, they have a room upstairs."

"Do they have an office anywhere else?"

"I don't know, sir," the clerk said, then added, "really."

"What room is theirs?"

"Sir—"

"Don't make me ask you again, son."

The clerk swallowed hard.

"It's room one, sir," he said, finally. "Room one, upstairs."

Clint looked around room one. It was a two-room suite, the largest in the hotel. It took him a long time to search it, and he wasn't careful about it. In the end it was an even bigger mess than the office, but he still hadn't found anything, not even an indication of what other properties they owned.

He stood in the center of the carnage. He had succeeded in sending a message to the Garvins, but hadn't succeeded in much more. They must have kept their records at some other location.

He left the room and went back downstairs to the lobby. This time the clerk had gotten smart and had vacated the premises. Clint went behind the desk and searched, but there was nothing there. He considered destroying the desk completely, but figured he'd done enough damage to send a message.

He turned and walked toward the door. At that moment a man and a woman came in together, carrying luggage. They stopped short when they saw Clint.

"Help you?" Clint asked.

"Uh, yes," the man said, "we'd like a room."

"Sure thing," Clint said, "why don't you just take any room in the place. On the house."

THIRTY-SEVEN

Clint went back to the Diamond Palace and found Lily in her office.

"We have to stop meeting like this," she said. "What's going on now?"

"I found out that Peter Forrest was in business with the Garvins."

"What?"

"They were his partners in the Lucky Lady," Clint said. "Lily, is there any chance that your husband was in business with them?"

"None."

"Are you sure?"

"If they owned part of this hotel," she said, "why would they be trying to buy it? Why not just come forward and show me the papers?"

"Good point."

"I have all my business papers here, in this desk," she said. "There is not a slip of paper with the Garvin name on it."

"That's good, then," he said.

"What's your next move?" she asked. "Going to see the Garvins?"

"I did that already," he said. "They weren't there."

"So what did you do?"

Clint shrugged and said, "I left them a message."

Clint and Lily went to the dining room. For some reason, they were both hungry—ravenous, in fact.

"What's your next move?" she asked, when they both had steak platters in front of them.

"I've been thinking about that," Clint said. "That building where the crate almost fell on you?"

"Yes."

"I want to find out who owns it."

"And how will you do that?"

"I'll have to get inside."

"But didn't you try that, already?"

"I did," he said, "but I didn't really try as hard as I could."

"And this time you will?"

"Oh, yes."

Over the meal he also told Lily that he was working with the police. He explained how Burns and Logan were working on the other murders.

"Looking to connect them?" she asked.

"I think it's all connected," he said. "It has to be."

"My husband's murder?"

"Yes."

"You mean . . . I'm actually going to find out who killed him?"

"If I have anything to say about it."

"I thought that was a lost cause."

"No lost causes, Lily," Clint said. "Not while we're alive to pursue them."

"I'm coming with you."

"No," he said, "you're staying here. I may have to move very quickly to get inside that building."

"Are you saying I can't move quickly?"

"I'm saying I can't afford to have to worry about you," Clint said. "I'm going to have enough problems worrying about myself."

"I want to be there when you find him," she said. "I want to see who killed my husband."

"You will be," he said.

"Promise?"

"I promise."

THIRTY-EIGHT

Clint returned to the place where Lily had almost been killed. But instead of going up to the building, he went across the street to the hardware store.

"Back again?" the clerk asked.

"I've got to get into that building across the street," Clint said. "And the doors are locked."

"Knock."

"Doesn't work."

"Break a window."

"Too noisy," Clint said. "I want to try to get in without being heard."

"What do you want from me?"

"A way in," Clint said. "A tool."

"Tool?"

"Something that will get me inside."

The man thought a moment, then walked away and returned carrying something.

"A crowbar," he said.

Clint took it.

"Thank you."

"Hey," the man said, as Clint turned to leave. Clint looked at him and the man put his hand out. "Pay me."

Clint crossed over to the building and walked along until he found an alley. It wouldn't do to put a crowbar to one of the front doors in broad daylight. He needed to find a side entry or a back entry. Door, window, it didn't matter.

He moved along the alley, found some windows that were too small or too high for him. He kept going until he got to the back of the building. There was room back there for deliveries, which meant buckboards and horse-drawn carts could pull right up to the building and unload. There were several doors to choose from, and windows.

He tried the doors first, just in case they were unlocked. Same with the windows. When he found them all locked, he went about choosing one that would be the easiest to pry open with the least noise.

He picked out a window that swung open from the top. All he had to do was slide the crowbar beneath the rim of the window and pry it open. He did so quietly, set the crowbar down on the ground, and climbed inside. He closed the window behind him.

He turned and looked at the room he was in. It was obviously storage, with crates and barrels all around him. They were unlabeled, so he had no idea what was in them, but it didn't matter. That wasn't what he was there for.

It was dim inside as he moved farther into the room, but his eyes adjusted quickly. The room was cavernous, with a high ceiling, but it wasn't large enough to take up the entire floor, so there were obviously others. And he could hear sounds above his head, which meant there were people on the second floor—the floor from which the crate had almost fallen on Lily.

Clint decided the downstairs was completely for storage, so he started looking for a stairway to the second floor. He found one at the end of the room to his far left. From here he could still hear sounds from upstairs, but now it included voices.

Cautiously, he started up the steps, hoping they would not creak beneath his weight. They didn't, and he made it to the top without incident. He was on the second floor, now, still storage. In fact, he felt he was looking at the window the crate had probably fallen—or been pushed—from. He could still hear voices, though, so he moved along toward them, trying to locate the offices.

Finally, he could see a door ahead of him with a light glowing beneath it. As he got closer the voices got louder.

He stopped right in front of the door.

". . . Had done your job right, we shouldn't be in this mess," a woman said. Christine Garvin, no doubt.

"Now, take it easy, Chris . . ." a man said. He didn't recognize the voice, but from the tone he assumed it was her husband, Harold Garvin.

"Why should I take it easy? This nitwit has put us in hot water from the start. How stupid was it to try to kill Lily Kingsforth with a goddamn crate."

"It seemed like a good idea, at the time," a deep male voice said.

"Well, it wasn't!" Chris Garvin said.

Clint listened until he was sure there were only three people in the room. Then he drew his gun, kicked in the door, and stepped into the room.

The Garvins were at one end of the room, near a desk. The other man—presumably the one with the deep voice—was closer to Clint. As the door flew open, the man turned and grabbed a gun from his belt.

"No!" Chris Garvin yelled, but it was too late.

Clint had no choice. He pulled the trigger once and put the man down.

THIRTY-NINE

"Don't shoot us!" Harold Garvin shouted, putting his hands out.

"Oh, Harold, relax," Christine said. "He only shot Zack because he had a gun. We don't have any weapons at all."

"Let's keep it that way," Clint said. "Keep your hands where I can see them." He holstered his gun as they obeyed, first replacing the round he had expended.

"This is the man who tried to kill Lily Kingsforth with a crate?" he asked.

"Ah, you were listening at the door," Christine said. "Yes, it was his brilliant idea."

Chris seemed calm while Harold, her mate, was sweating and looked as if he was going to faint. He was very pale, and Clint didn't know if that was his normal pallor or not. He had narrow shoulders, a prominent Adam's apple, and listless, sparse brown hair. To Clint they made a very odd couple. He wondered why Harold conducted all the business when it seemed Chris had all the backbone.

"What's this all about?" Chris asked. "Lily, or more than that?"

"Oh, more," Clint said. "Much more. Try Peter Forrest's murder."

"What do we have to do with that?" she demanded.

"You were his partners," Clint said, "at least, in the Lucky Lady. So now you own it."

"So? That doesn't make us murderers."

"What I'm interested in is who else you're partners with."

"Why?" Chris asked. "What business is it of yours?"

"I'm working with the police to solve three—no, four—other murders counting Walter Trench's and Paul Kingsforth's."

"Four?" Harold asked. He looked at his wife. "What the hell is he talking about?"

"How should I know?" she snapped back.

Clint wondered why Harold would think his wife would know.

"Kingsforth, that's crazy," she said, looking at Clint. "That was years ago, and he was robbed on the street."

"I'm not so sure it was robbery," Clint said.

"And who the hell is Walter Trench?" she demanded.

"A Pinkerton agent," he said.

"What would we know about a Pinkerton agent?" she asked.

"Well, if your business is not so legal, I guess you'd be interested in him," Clint said, "or in getting rid of him."

"Look," she said, "we've got nothing to say and unless you have a badge, you can't stop us from leaving."

"You own this building?"

"So what?" she asked.

"Just answer the question."

"We own it."

"Then you can go," he said. "I'm sure I can find the records I'm looking for in these files."

There were several file cabinets in the room. This was obviously where the Garvins kept their business records.

Harold looked around, nervously.

"You can't go through our files," he said.

"Why not?"

"You—you're not the law."

"So stop me," Clint said, putting his hand on his gun. The move caused Harold to flinch.

"You—you're a killer," he said. "You killed Zack for no reason."

"I killed him because he went for his gun," Clint said. "I can kill you and stick a gun in your belt and claim you threw down on me, too. What do you think of that, Harold?"

Harold's eyes popped.

"Y-you wouldn't."

"Of course he wouldn't," Chris told her husband. "He's bluffing just to scare you, and it's working."

"W-we have to get out of here," Harold said.

"So go," she said, folding her arms. "I'm staying right here. Mr. Adams is gonna have to go through me to see these files."

"Sure, go ahead, Harold," Clint said. "Leave. I get the feeling you're not the businessman everybody thinks you are. I think you're the front for your wife's brilliant business mind."

"C-Chris—" Harold stammered.

"He's right, Harold," she said. "Get out." She settled

her pert butt on top of the desk and regarded Clint from beneath heavy lids. "Mr. Adams and I have some business to discuss."

"B-business—"

"Yes, business, Harold," she said. "Damn it, pull yourself together and get out. Wait for me at home."

"Home being the hotel on the Coast?" Clint asked. "Yeah, you might have some cleaning up to do there, Harold."

"What are you—"

"Go home, Harold," Chris said. "Now!"

Looking like he was going to cry, Harold slid past Clint and went out the door.

"Okay," Clint said, "now what?"

"I don't know about you," Chris said, "but I suddenly feel like having sex right here on this desk."

"Christine—"

"Maybe it's seeing you shoot somebody?" she asked, undoing the top buttons of the simple dress she was wearing. Clint had the feeling that was what she had been wearing when the desk clerk told them he was at their hotel, and she hadn't had time to change when she and her husband ran out the back. And then they had come straight here.

To do what?

"What do you think?"

Clint had allowed his attention to wander for just a minute. A sign of age, he thought. Luckily, rather than grabbing a gun from her desk, Christine Garvin had simply dropped all of her clothes to the floor.

FORTY

"You're crazy," Clint said to her. "Get dressed."

She laughed.

"Make me."

He approached her, leaning over to pick up her clothes. She kicked them away before he could pick them up, then wrapped her naked body around him. Her breasts were large and firm, her skin hot, the scent of her heady. He knew if he put his hand between her legs, he'd find her wet and ready. He also knew if he did that, he'd be lost.

"Chris, stop—" He tried to disentangle himself from her but she held on tight. She slid her hand between them, cupped his crotch, and laughed again.

"Oh, my," she said, "you're as ready as I am. Why fight it?"

"Chris—" She silenced him with a kiss. She pushed her tongue into his mouth as she rubbed his crotch. He put his hand on one of her thighs to try to pull her leg off of him, but his hand slid along her smooth flesh, and suddenly he was cupping her crotch.

He was right about two things.

She was sticky wet and ready.

And he was lost.

Together they pulled off his clothes, and then he lifted her onto the desk. This was a first for him, having sex with a woman with a dead man in the room. A lot of firsts for him this trip to San Francisco.

He spread her legs and bulled himself into her, and she urged him on as he fucked her. Apparently, having a dead body in the room had them both excited, both thrusting against each other in an attempt to achieve their own pleasure. At one point they were just two bodies writhing together, making the temperature in the room rise. He felt her explode beneath him when he was just moments from his own climax. He groaned and exploded into her, and although they didn't begin the ascent at the same time, they did come down from it together.

He had removed his holster and put in on the desk. Now he reached out and slammed his hand down on top of hers just before she could draw the gun from the holster.

"You're a cold bitch," he said, climbing off her and picking up the holster.

She drew her legs up and stared at him, smiling.

"Don't kid yourself," she said. "I did want to fuck you, but yeah, then I was gonna kill you."

"And that didn't work," he said, gathering up his clothes. He moved across the room from her to dress. As he was pulling his trousers on she turned over onto her belly, showing him her ass. It was a great ass, but it wasn't worth dying over. He heard the top drawer of the desk open and as she turned over with the gun, bringing it to bear on him, he drew his gun and shot her. Her body jumped as the bullet struck her, and she made a sound like "oh." A look of surprise came over her face, and then she dropped the gun she was holding and slumped onto her side on top of the desk.

Clint finished putting his boots on and then strapped on the holster before walking across the room to check her. She was as dead as she could be.

He backed away from her and replaced the spent shell in his gun with a live one. He stood staring at the two bodies, one on the floor, the other on the desk, wondering how he was going to explain this to Burns and Logan. After all, she *was* naked.

He could have just walked and not called the police, but the clerk in the hardware store could identify him. He'd tell the police the story about the man who came in to get a crowbar.

No, he was going to have to call the police, but first he decided to have a look around.

He searched through the files and found many sets of partnership papers. Apparently, the Garvins were partners with many people—senior partners, from the way the paperwork read.

The dead man on the floor, who they had called "Zack," was their partner in this building. His name was Zackary Bolden.

That name struck Clint as being familiar. He didn't find it on any other papers, but he did find some papers with a company name on them. That is, it wasn't a man's name listed as partners with the Garvins, but a company called House of Cards Holding Company.

Zackary Bolden . . . okay, yeah, now he remembered

where he had seen the name. And he remembered that he'd been told that Bolden was already dead—which, obviously, had been a lie.

He was going to have to have a talk with the man behind the House of Cards Holding Company, and he knew just where to find him.

But first, the police.

FORTY-ONE

The office was busy with policemen, both in uniform and out of uniform. As the bodies were carried from the room, Burns and Logan stood aside with Clint. Lieutenant Hargrove came walking over to them.

"Naked? On the desk?" he asked.

"That's right," Clint said.

Hargrove shook his head.

"Are you going to tell me she had sex with the guy on the floor, who's not her husband?"

"Okay," Clint said, thinking that sounded good so far.

"And you walked in on them."

"Yeah."

"The man pulled a gun, you shot him."

"Right."

"The naked woman pulled a gun."

"Yes."

"From where?" he asked. "She was naked."

"Top desk drawer."

Burns opened the drawer, looked inside.

"Got some gun oil stains in here, Lieutenant," he said.

"So she pulls a gun from the drawer and you've got no choice but to shoot her."

"Right."

"Don't you do some of that trick shooting?" Logan asked. "Couldn't you have, like, hit her in the shoulder?"

"I don't do trick shooting when my life's on the line," Clint said. "This isn't like shooting at targets, Inspector."

"Hey, I was just askin'," Logan said. "You say that's what happened, I believe you."

The other policemen followed the body out, carrying boxes of files, and then Hargrove closed the door so that it was only the four of them inside.

"Where were you two?" he asked his inspectors.

"We were pursuing other leads, sir," Burns said.

"What leads?"

"We decided to split up, work the three murders as if they were separate."

Hargrove looked at Clint.

"You sure you're not a detective? You talk like one."

"I have a lot of friends who are detectives," Clint said, "and lawmen."

Hargrove stared at the three men in turn, then asked, "Okay, whaddaya got?"

"What do you mean?"

"I mean, you've got something," Hargrove said, "I can see it."

He looked at Burns.

"I was working Eddie MacDonald," Burns said. "I found out he had partners."

"Who?"

"The Garvins."

"Partners in a dump like that?"

"Look at all the paperwork in these files," Clint said. "They were partners with a lot of people."

"Like who?"

"Peter Forrest."

"Dead," Burns said.

"And Paul Kingsforth."

"Dead," Logan said.

"And Eddie MacDonald," Hargrove said, "also dead. Do they have any partners who are still alive?"

"Yes," Clint said, "a lot."

"Well, I guess they should be warned," the lieutenant said, "if these people are going around killing their partners."

"We don't know that, yet," Clint said.

"What?"

"They could have a partner who's killing their partners."

"Like I said," Hargrove responded, "what've you got?"

"Something I still have to check on," Clint said. "And then I may have all of the answers."

Hargrove regarded him curiously.

"You know, by rights what I should do is take away your gun and put you in a cell."

"But you won't because you believe me, right?"

"I believe you about him," Hargrove said, "but not necessarily her."

"Look," Clint said, "all we need is for Burns and Logan to go and get Harold Garvin and bring him in."

"And you?"

"I told you," Clint said. "I have one more thing to do."

Hargrove took a deep breath and blew it out.

"Okay," he said, "but I'm not going to lose my job over this. Come back to me with something solid, or I'm tossing you into a cell, Gunsmith or no Gunsmith."

"I've got it," Clint said.

"Okay, then let's get out of here."

Outside Hargrove told them all to be in his office in two hours.

"I don't get it," Inspector Logan said, as his boss walked away.

"Don't get what?" Inspector Burns asked.

"Adams," Logan said, "why didn't you just walk away, make it look like they shot each other?"

"Because they didn't," Clint said, "and that wouldn't solve anything."

Both men stared at him.

"And the man in the hardware store knew I was here," Clint said.

"Okay," Logan said, "that makes sense."

"You sure you don't want one of us to come with you?" Burns asked.

"No," Clint said, "I want to do this part alone."

"What about Walter Trench?" Logan asked. "I couldn't find anything on the Pinkerton."

"Did you talk to his partner?"

"Can't find her."

"Okay," Clint said, "I'll talk to her."

"You think Trench was involved with all this?"

"I think we've linked all the other murders," Clint said. "Why not his?"

"You gonna make it to the boss's office in two hours?" Burns asked.

"I'll be there," Clint said.

"Okay," Burns said, and then to his partner added, "let's go get the husband."

FORTY-TWO

Clint entered the House of Cards and went right to the bar. Business was starting to pick up as gamblers who had jobs during the day joined the gamblers who had no jobs.

"I need to see your boss," he said to the bartender, Wesley.

"He's in his office."

"Okay, thanks." Clint started away, then stopped short. "Is he alone?"

Wesley shrugged. "As far as I know."

Clint decided to chance walking in on Frank Ellington interviewing a prospective female employee.

He walked down the long hall to the office and knocked on the door.

"Come in."

He opened the door and stuck his head in. "You alone?"

Ellington laughed from behind his desk.

"Come on in, Clint."

Clint entered, then closed the door behind him. He

wondered if Harold Garvin had gotten to Ellington with news.

"How goes your business in San Francisco?"

"It's starting to come together," Clint said. "Just today I killed two people."

"Is that a fact?"

"Yep," Clint said. "You'll be interested to know one of them was Zack Bolden."

"Why would that interest me?"

"Because you told me Zack Bolden was already dead, remember?"

"Oh."

"And the other one might interest you, too," Clint said. "A partner of yours."

"Partner?"

"Christine Garvin."

Ellington's eyes went wide.

"You killed Christine?"

"Had to," Clint said. "She was trying to kill him."

"What about—"

"Harold? He ran off. The police are tracking him down, now."

Ellington didn't look happy.

"Don't look so worried," Clint said. "The police don't need Harold to tie you to the Garvins and to the murders."

"What are you talking about?"

"They've got the contracts," Clint went on, "the partnership agreements linking the Garvins to House of Cards Holding. That's you, right?"

Ellington frowned unhappily.

"It's over, Frank," Clint said. "You've been killing or having your partners killed. I'll bet we find papers linking you to Peter Forrest, Paul Kingsforth—what about Adrian Webster? Was he next?"

"No," a cultured voice said from behind him, "you are next, Mr. Adams."

Clint stiffened. "Adrian?"

"I have a pistol pointed at your back."

"Where did you come from?"

"A little hallway behind that wall," Ellington said. "It's my back way out, but you couldn't see it when you walked in. When you knocked, Adrian ducked back there."

Clint felt his gun being lifted from his holster. Going to the warehouse had been the first time he'd worn the holster in San Francisco. It had saved his life twice already that day.

Funny, third time was usually the charm.

Not today.

FORTY-THREE

"What do we do with him?" Ellington asked.

"Take him down the back," Webster said, "and get rid of him."

"I'll have Kenny—"

"No," Webster said. "No Kenny. We do this ourselves, to make sure it's done right. Killing Trench was sloppy, just as killing Kingsforth was. Adams, here, did us a favor if he really killed Zack and Christine. That only leaves Harold."

"And maybe Harold will take the fall for it all," Ellington said.

"Maybe," Adrian said. "That's good thinking. But right now we need to get rid of Mr. Adams."

Ellington opened the top drawer of his desk and took out a Colt. He stood up and tucked it into his belt.

"What would Rick say, Frank?" Clint asked.

"Leave Rick out of this, Adams," Ellington said. "He does business his way, I do it mine. Now move."

Clint turned. Adrian Webster was smart enough to

move away from him. He jerked the gun toward the hidden doorway and Clint moved.

"Takes us to a back door," Ellington said, from behind. "Nowhere to run when we get outside, if that's what you're thinking."

That wasn't what Clint was thinking. He was thinking about the New Line tucked into the small of his back. He just needed some space to make the move. Drawing from behind your back needs more elbow room than drawing from a holster.

When they reached the door Webster said, "Open it, and step out."

"Business is starting to pick up," Ellington said. "Nobody inside will hear anything."

Clint considered pressing the matter in the hall, but they were keeping their distance. He opened the door and stepped out.

He heard a hammer cock, and as Adrian Webster came out the door, one shot. Then the sound of a bullet striking flesh. Clint stepped to the side, went down to one knee, and reached behind him, beneath his jacket, for the New Line. As Ellington came out the door, he stopped as Webster fell in front of him. Confused, Ellington looked at Clint just as the New Line came out and lined up on him. Eyes wide, Ellington went for the gun in his belt.

Clint pulled the trigger on the New Line three times, because it was a .32 and Frank Ellington was a big man.

He wondered how he would tell Rick Hartman that he had killed his friend.

Clint collected his gun from Adrian Webster's body. Kat Crawford came walking over, her gun still held out in front of her.

"Did they kill Walter?" she asked.

"Yes," Clint said, "they had him killed."

"By who?"

"We may never know that," Clint said, "but whoever did it was like the trigger on a gun. It was these two men who pulled the trigger."

"Why?"

"They were trying to take over."

"Take what over?"

"All the businesses they were partners in," Clint said. "They've been killing all their partners, starting with Paul Kingsforth two years ago."

"How can you prove it?"

"Paperwork," Clint said, "and the partner who's left, Harold Garvin. I don't think it'll take too much to get him talking."

"So what do we do?"

"I have an appointment with the police," Clint said. "You come with me and we'll lay it all out."

"What do we do with them?"

"We just leave them here," Clint said. "The police will collect them."

"So it's all over?" she asked.

"It's over," he said, "except for the explanations."

Lily would have to be told that her husband was partners with the others—if she really didn't know. Either way she'd be in business for herself from now on.

They turned and started walking away from the bodies to the street.

"Hey," she said, stopping.

"What?"

"What about Allan Pinkerton's death?" she asked. "Weren't we supposed to find something out about that?"

"No," Clint said, "I don't think we were. I think that whole story was just a way to get me here."

"Doesn't that make you mad?" she asked. "Being used like that?"

"Oh, yes," he said. "It does; it makes me very mad."

But that was something he was going to have to deal with later.

AUTHOR'S NOTE

Portsmouth Square (Chinese: 花園角) is a one-block park in Chinatown, San Francisco, California, that is bounded by Kearny Street on the east, Washington Street on the north, Clay Street on the south, and Walter Lum Place on the west.

There was the Parker House, originally built by its owner, Robert A. Parker, as a hotel, but quickly converted to a casino as the gambling craze swept San Francisco. A large room downstairs contained three tables for faro, two for monte, one for roulette, and a seventh for any other game desired. Professional gamblers paid ten thousand dollars a month for the privilege of conducting their games in this room. A smaller room behind the bar went for thirty-five hundred dollars a month. Jack Gamble, an appropriately named sporting man, leased the entire second floor for sixty thousand dollars and outfitted all the rooms for games of chance. It was estimated that at the peak of the California Gold Rush upward of half a million dollars was stacked on the tables of the Parker House on any given day.

Flanking the Parker House on either side were two other famous resorts, Samuel Dennison's Exchange and the El Dorado Gambling Saloon, owned by partners James McCabe and Thomas J. A. Chambers. Other houses on Portsmouth Square were the Verandah, the Aguila de Oro, the Bella Union, the Empire, the Arcade, the Varsouvienne, the Mazourka, the Ward House, the St. Charles, the Alhambra, La Souciedad, the Fontine House, and the Rendezvous. As indicated by the several French names, some of these establishments were owned and operated by gambling syndicates from France, a country long known for its love of gaming.

Watch for

PARIAH

337th novel in the exciting GUNSMITH series
from Jove

Coming in January!

J GIANT ACTION! GIANT ADVENTURE!

THE GUNSMITH

J.R. ROBERTS

penguin.com/actionwesterns

M455AS0509

LONGARM

GIANT-SIZED ADVENTURE FROM AVENGING ANGEL LONGARM.

BY TABOR EVANS

2006 Giant Edition:

LONGARM AND THE OUTLAW EMPRESS

2007 Giant Edition:

LONGARM AND THE GOLDEN EAGLE SHOOT-OUT

2008 Giant Edition:

LONGARM AND THE VALLEY OF SKULLS

2009 Giant Edition:

LONGARM AND THE LONE STAR TRACKDOWN

penguin.com/actionwesterns